There's trouble ahead for Katie

Christina drew in a long, steady breath and then breathed out slowly. The faint white scar that cut through her left eyebrow became noticeable, the way it always did when she furrowed her brow with concern.

"What?" Katie asked impatiently.

"I know you hate to hear this kind of stuff," Christina began carefully, "but I think you should go home right away."

"Why?" Katie asked. "And what kind of stuff are you talking about?"

"You know, my ESP feelings. I know you think it's crazy, but—"

"Yes, I think it's crazy," Katie abruptly cut in. Yet, this time, despite her skepticism, a cold chill of fear ran up Katie's spine.

The Golden Angel

FOREVER ANGELS

The Golden Angel

Suzanne Weyn

Troll

Text copyright © 1996 by Chardiet Unlimited, Inc., and Suzanne Weyn.
Cover illustration copyright © 1996 by Mark English.
Cover border photography by Katrina.
Angel stickers (5500-0019) copyright © 1996 by Gallery Graphics, Inc., Noel, MO 64854. Used with permission.

Published by Troll Communications L.L.C.

Printed in the United States of America.

10   9   8   7   6   5   4   3   2   1

For my sister, Anne M. Maloney, with love

The Golden Angel

1

"I don't know about this," Katie Nelson said with a worried scowl. "Do you think they can handle it?"

Her sharp amber eyes scanned the sunny dayroom, taking in the fifteen or so children in various colored bathrobes. They sat in friendly clusters at the three child-sized pinewood tables. Some spoke to one another in serious whispers. Others giggled. Most worked with quiet concentration on the brightly colored clay they molded in their small, quick hands.

The pretty, long-legged blond girl beside her followed Katie's gaze around the room. "They're not too sick to sing," Christina disagreed, sweeping her thick wheat-colored hair back behind her broad shoulders. "You saw their faces when we sang with them this morning. It's magical. They're so happy they look like angels."

Katie looked hard and meaningfully at Christina. "Like angels?" Katie questioned, arching her brow.

"Well, you know what I mean," Christina said. "They look beautiful. They glow."

"Oh," Katie said. "I thought maybe you'd seen something . . . something else."

"No. Oh, no," Christina said quickly. "I didn't mean *that*. I was only using 'like angels' as an expression." She leaned close and whispered. "I haven't actually seen an angel around here. Not lately."

"Oh. I was wondering," Katie said as she tucked a loose strand of her shoulder-length auburn hair into the baseball cap she wore brim-backward. After everything she, Christina, and their friends Ashley and Molly had experienced, she was always alert for the presence of actual angels.

The sick children at Children's House—a homey old Victorian house for young patients from the pediatric ward in the main hospital—were certainly sweet. But did they really look like angels when they sang?

In a way, yes.

When they sang together in a group, their innocent faces glowed with an inner light, all sickness and fear forgotten for the moment. Ever since Katie and Christina started volunteering at Children's House, they'd met a lot of sick children whose bravery and spirit had touched their hearts. They were certainly the closest things to little angels that Katie could think of, even the mischievous ones.

"Still, I'm not sure about this show idea of yours," Katie said, facing Christina. "What did Ms. Baker say?"

A petite woman with a friendly face and short gray hair stepped between Katie and Christina. "What did I say about what?" she questioned with a smile.

"Hi, Ms. Baker." Christina greeted the woman. "Did

you think about my idea for the show over at the nursing home? Don't you think the people there would love it?"

Ms. Baker, who was in charge of the volunteer program at Children's House, nodded, her expression thoughtful and serious. "Yes, I'm sure they would. It would be good for the kids, too. Doing something for others brings them out of themselves. Helping others is empowering for them. It makes them feel strong and capable instead of small and sick."

Christina clapped her hands together in delight, and her large, sky-blue eyes brightened. "Then we can do it?"

"Yes," Ms. Baker said.

"Are you sure the kids aren't too sick?" Katie worried aloud.

"We'll need parental permission, of course," Ms. Baker said. "But the kids who are really weak are over in the pediatric ward of the main hospital. Our kids could handle singing. I assume you won't have them doing circus stunts or cartwheels, or anything like that."

"No way." Christina laughed. "We won't do anything too wild. I promise."

"Fine then. I don't see any problem," Ms. Baker agreed. "I'll call the Pine Ridge Nursing Home and ask them when they'd want you to come. Don't tell the kids until I get the go-ahead from the nursing home, all right?"

"Sure thing," Christina agreed.

As Katie watched Ms. Baker leave, a small hand tugged on the hem of her blue fleece top. "Katie, could you help me?" asked an adorable five-year-old girl with black hair and almond-shaped eyes.

"Sure, Chu-Lian. What's the problem?" Katie replied, smiling down at the anxiously frowning child.

"My angel's wings keep falling off," she explained as she led Katie to her place at one of the tables. On the table sat a six-inch angel made of blue clay.

"Wow, this is good," Katie said sincerely. Chu-Lian definitely had artistic talent. The head, torso, and wide cone-shaped skirt of her angel were well formed. "This is *really* good!"

"But look at the wings," Chu-Lian fretted, pointing to two wing-shaped pieces of clay on the table. "No matter what I do, they won't stay on."

"Why don't you just make it a human girl without wings?" Katie suggested.

Chu-Lian shook her head firmly. "It has to be an angel."

"Why?"

"Because when I was having my operation, I saw an angel. It was after the doctor gave me the sleeping medicine. The angel held my hand the whole time. She was *soooo* beautiful. And her hands were really, really soft. So was her voice."

Katie pulled out a child-sized chair and sat at the low table. She studied Chu-Lian's innocent eyes. "What else do you remember about the angel?" Katie asked seriously.

"She had long, straight black hair and her eyes were strange—kind of purplish blue. She was really, really tall, with humongous shining wings."

"You saw an angel, all right," Katie said quietly. Chu-Lian's description fit the angels Katie had seen. The height. Those eyes. Though the angels could look very different, they were all tall, winged, and had striking eyes.

"I know I saw an angel," Chu-Lian replied. "I just told you I did."

Katie smiled. "Yes, you did," she said. "Well, let's see what I can do here with these wings." She pressed the blue clay together in her hands. "I bet I can get these on."

"You believe me about the angel, don't you?" Chu-Lian asked eagerly.

"Oh, yes," Katie replied, still working the clay. "Most definitely."

"My mother doesn't," Chu-Lian said, putting her hands on the table and resting her head on them. "Neither does my father. They say it was only a nice dream. My brother says believing in angels is for babies."

"They're wrong," Katie said without hesitation. If they only knew *how* wrong. Carefully, she attached the edge of a wing near the figure's shoulder blade. The wings wouldn't stay on because Chu-Lian had made them very large, and their weight and size pulled them down. Katie didn't want to make them smaller, though. She knew the girl had formed the wings accurately, just exactly as she'd seen them.

"How do you know so much about angels?" Chu-Lian asked, her head still resting comfortably on her hands.

"Because I've seen angels myself."

Chu-Lian's eyes widened in awe. "You have?"

Katie nodded. "And I only believe in things I can see with my own eyes. If I can't see it, I don't believe it. But I actually saw angels, so I'm sure they're real."

"Where did you see them?" Chu-Lian asked.

"All around. Everywhere. I sometimes see them on an old covered bridge in the Pine Manor woods. There's no sign, but I know it's called the Angels Crossing Bridge because I found the old sign from the bridge in my uncle's barn. Sometimes I see angels there, and other times I just see them around. I was younger than you the first time I ever saw one."

"You were?"

"Yep. I was riding my bike down a path and I couldn't stop. I would have crashed into the street and right into a car if a beautiful lady with wings hadn't stopped me. She stood right in my path and kept me from going into the road, and then she disappeared."

Katie used her thumbs to secure the second wing onto the clay angel. Her memory of this event was so clear, as if it had happened yesterday. "My parents didn't believe me, either."

"Do they believe you now that you're big?" Chu-Lian asked hopefully. "I bet they do!"

Without meaning to, Katie's thumb twitched, knocking off the second wing. "Darn!" she snapped.

"Now that you're big, do they believe you?" Chu-Lian pressed. She obviously hoped that someday, with age, her parents would believe her, too.

"Well," Katie said carefully, "maybe they do believe me now. I think they must."

"Did they say so?"

"Not exactly," Katie replied. "I haven't seen my parents since last year. They're dead."

Chu-Lian sat up and put her small hand on Katie's arm in a gesture of heartfelt sympathy. The child's innocent, genuine comforting brought an unexpected, unwelcome lump to Katie's throat.

No matter how many times she told herself she was moving on with her life—that her parents' death in a car accident was no longer an open wound, bleeding inside her heart—something always came along to prove otherwise. A small, intimate exchange like this could suddenly, unexpectedly, undo her hard-won calm.

A tear rolled down her cheek, and Katie wiped it away briskly. This was no time for crying, especially not in front of a little girl who had serious problems of her own. The operation on Chu-Lian's kidney had hopefully been successful, but they wouldn't know for certain until her tests came back.

"Those wings look like they'll stay put now," Katie said in a husky, low voice. She forced the tone of her voice up a level to make it more cheerful. "It's a beautiful angel."

Christina came up behind Katie and put her hand on her shoulder. "Can I talk to you a minute," she said seriously.

"Sure," Katie replied, getting to her feet. She walked to the corner of the room with Christina. "What's up?"

Christina drew in a long, steady breath and then breathed out slowly. The faint white scar that cut through her left eyebrow became noticeable, the way it always did when she furrowed her brow with concern.

"What?" Katie asked impatiently. Christina's seriousness was worrying her. "What's up?"

"I know you hate to hear this kind of stuff," Christina began carefully, "but I think you should go home right away."

"Why?" Katie asked. "And what kind of stuff are you talking about?"

"My kind of stuff. You know, my ESP feelings. I know you think it's crazy but—"

"Yes. I think it's crazy," Katie abruptly cut in. Christina could be so flaky sometimes! All her talk about mystical power, dreams, tarot, horoscope, and all the rest drove Katie crazy. It was so wacky!

Yet, this time, despite her skepticism, a cold chill of fear ran up Katie's spine.

In the past, Christina had been right about so many things. There was no denying that. Katie always attributed her success to luck and coincidence. But, still . . . something inside Katie—a more superstitious, more mystical place in her mind—wondered. Maybe Christina really did have an extra sense, a sixth sense that helped her know things.

"Why should I go home?" Katie challenged.

"I don't know why," Christina admitted fretfully. "I just have a feeling you should. Every time I look at you, I feel worried."

"Oh, thanks a lot," Katie joked.

"I'm not kidding," Christina insisted as the white scar seemed to deepen on her brow.

2

I'm as nuts as she is, Katie grumbled to herself as she got off the bus. *Why did I even listen to her? I must be crazy.*

Yet something in Christina's words had worked on Katie's doubting nature. At Christina's urging, she'd left Children's House and hopped on Pine Ridge public bus number five. The bus brought her from the hospital to a stop on a country road not far from the house she lived in with her Uncle Jeff, Aunt Rainie, and twenty-year-old cousin, Mel.

Katie stepped off the bus and shivered. Yanking the collar of her fleece-lined denim jacket forward, she looked around at the vibrant colors of the changing autumn leaves. It was beautiful here in Pine Ridge. There was no doubt about that.

It was so different from the city where she'd grown up. Here, autumn trees—colorful oaks and maples— lived alongside huge, lush, ancient, and unchanging evergreens; mountains seemed to ramble on forever, growing a faint purple as they receded into the distance; and long stretches of open grazing fields and farmland were generously low, revealing wide, clear skies that the trees and mountains obscured. At first, she thought she'd never get used to these surroundings. But she had.

She'd even come to love them.

Had she come to love Aunt Rainie, Uncle Jeff, and Mel, too? She wondered about this as she began walking up the long, pine tree–lined stone and dirt road that led to their old, weathered house.

Certainly she appreciated that they'd brought her to live with them after her parents' death. She knew it was an unselfish thing to do. It wasn't easy for them, either. They surely weren't rich, far from it.

Even though Katie considered Aunt Rainie super ditzy, she was also kind and loving. Uncle Jeff could be a pain, always griping about money, rarely smiling, but he was never unkind. Mel was definitely a super drag. All he ever thought about was himself, his motorcycle, and his girl-friend, Mary Ellen, in that order. He barely acknowledged Katie's presence at all. She did like his black dog, Dizzy, though. Lately Dizzy and she had grown to be friends.

They were okay, really. Not the worst people on earth at all.

But did she *love* them?

"I don't know," she whispered aloud. What did love feel like? She wasn't sure. She'd loved her parents but had taken that love for granted, never noticing the way it felt. Stopping, she closed her eyes and tried to think about how she'd felt with her parents.

Safe?

Happy?

Connected?

Yes. She'd felt all those things.

Did she feel those things now? She definitely felt safe. Her aunt and uncle were good people.

Happy? Sometimes.

Connected? That was the hard one.

No. She didn't feel connected to them, not even to Aunt Rainie. Not in the way she'd been connected to her parents. It simply wasn't the same.

Katie swallowed hard. The truth was surprisingly uncomfortable. Jamming her hands into her pockets, she bent her head against the cold wind stirring the trees.

Walking several paces, she stopped, lifted her chin, and sniffed the chill air. What was the sweet, smoky smell drifting toward her? Was someone burning leaves? Was it a fire from a fireplace?

She looked around. Their nearest neighbor was several acres away. Should she be able to smell their fireplace from here? It didn't seem like she should.

Continuing down the road, Katie's mind went back to thinking about family. She had a family. Yet she didn't. She was oddly in between, and it didn't feel good.

Why did my parents have to take that stupid vacation? she wondered bitterly. *If they'd stayed home, they'd never have been in that car accident. They'd have been home with me in our apartment. Maybe they'd still be alive.*

Something in the air made Katie lift her head sharply. That smell again. Only stronger now.

"Oh, no!" she shouted.

A cloud of thick, black smoke climbed into the air in front of her. It was coming from her house!

3

Katie raced back out to the main road, waving her arms at passing cars, shouting for help. She needed someone to call the Pine Ridge fire department—and fast!

A state police patrol car happened to pass. It pulled over. Katie raced to the driver's window and spoke to the balding officer in rapid, gasping words. "Fire . . . fire . . . at my house . . . back there," she panted, pointing back at the cloud of smoke that coiled up into the sky, swirling above the majestic pines.

The officer peered into the sky. He picked up his car radio and contacted the fire department. "They'll be here any moment," he told Katie.

"Thank you! Thank you so much!" Katie said, relieved that help was on its way.

The officer nodded. "Good luck," he said.

She glanced at the silver nameplate above the breast pocket of his blue uniform. OFFICER WI was all she could see. "Officer Winger!" Katie whispered as the police car sped away. She had met police officers with that name before, and she was certain they were angels.

In seconds, the urgent wail of a fire siren filled the air. Soon, the bright red hook-and-ladder truck of the Pine Ridge Volunteer Fire Department raced into view.

Katie waved at them, swinging her arms wide, directing them down the dirt road toward her house. Its siren still screaming, the truck careened around the corner and sped to the house.

Coming in right behind the truck, Aunt Rainie screeched into the dirt road in her beat-up old car.

"Katie, honey, the police called me at work. What happened?" she asked after pulling to a sharp stop and throwing open the passenger-side door to let Katie in.

"I don't know," Katie said as she climbed in beside Aunt Rainie. "But the house is definitely on fire!"

"My kitchen!" Aunt Rainie wailed, her plump hands covering her cheeks. "My kitchen!"

With a crash, a firefighter's ax smashed through the char-blackened door. Volunteer firefighters in long black and yellow coats moved with precise, well-practiced efficiency, some working the high-pressure hose, aiming its stream at the flames that licked up from the roof; others hacking at the house with axes, opening holes from which curling black smoke poured.

"How could this have happened?" Aunt Rainie asked with tears in her eyes. Her broad face and tightly permed blond hair were spotted with the soot that floated freely in the air. Her cheerful, bright, lime green pantsuit seemed sadly out of place in this unhappy scene.

Katie grabbed Aunt Rainie's wrist. "Dizzy!" she cried sharply, suddenly realizing she hadn't seen Mel's dog. "Where's Dizzy?"

Aunt Rainie's blue eyes widened in concern. She strained her soft round neck forward, searching for him. "Maybe he's with Mel," she said hopefully.

Not likely, Katie thought. For one thing, Mel's precious motorcycle was gone. He couldn't have taken Dizzy on that. And, besides, Mel usually left Dizzy in the house when he went out.

Katie began running back and forth, looking for Dizzy. She knew she'd let her young cat, Nagle, out before leaving the house, and Myrtle, Nagle's mother, stayed in the old barn behind the house. But where was Dizzy?

As she searched, Katie spotted Hank Kingsley, her friend Ashley's father. He was a volunteer firefighter. "Mr. Kingsley!" she called. "There's a dog in there, I think."

He gave a businesslike wave as he hurried toward the house. "I'll look," he called back before disappearing through the hacked-open doorway.

"Oh, my lord!" Aunt Rainie cried out in alarm as the kitchen wall collapsed forward. Flakes of charred wood filled the air as it banged to the ground.

With the wall down, Katie could see the kitchen. It was completely black. The sink, oven, and refrigerator were scorched. Then she saw Mr. Kingsley stand up from behind the remains of the overturned kitchen table. In his arms, he cradled a large black dog.

"Dizzy!" Katie cried, running to meet Mr. Kingsley as he walked out of the house with the dog.

"He was under the table. His heart's beating," Mr. Kingsley reported when Katie reached him. "The smoke probably got him. I'll send a medic over with some oxygen for the big guy." He laid Dizzy down on the grass near Aunt Rainie and then walked toward the fire truck.

Katie knelt beside Dizzy and petted his fur. Her hand came up black with soot. "His heart's beating," she said, looking up at Aunt Rainie, who was watching her.

Aunt Rainie crouched beside Katie. "Poor thing," she murmured, petting the dog.

One of the firefighters came running toward them with a small canister of oxygen and a mask. He gently placed the mask over Dizzy's nose and mouth, then turned the oxygen on. Several nervous minutes ticked by. Then, with a low whimper, Dizzy's brown eyes slowly opened.

"Good boy!" Katie cried with delight, ruffling the fur between his drooping ears. "Good boy!"

"Crazy dog," Aunt Rainie said fondly as she patted his side. "He'll probably be dizzier than ever, now that his head's been filled with smoke." She looked up at Katie. "Thank goodness you came home when you did or he'd be dead—and the entire house would be burned to the ground."

Katie nodded. "I know," she said quietly. Christina had done it again. Katie wasn't sure how. Did she have ESP, extrasensory perception, the ability to know things before they happened? Or had an angel whispered in her ear? Maybe Christina was just very alert to their messages, even from a distance.

Katie looked up the road and saw an old Jeep racing toward them at full speed. It screeched to a stop, and a tall, powerfully built man leaped from the Jeep. His deeply lined, leathery face was alive with panic. "Rainie, what happened?" he cried, throwing his arms wide. "What happened here?"

Katie pressed her lips into a tight line. Couldn't he see what had happened? The old fool!

She knew what he really meant, though. He was asking who was to blame for this. Uncle Jeff was big on assigning blame for things. It was the trait she liked least about him. He always did it when he was upset, and he was *very* upset now.

"I don't know, Jeff," Aunt Rainie shouted at him. "I was at work, and some police officer called me."

Officer Winger, Katie added silently.

Uncle Jeff looked sharply at Katie.

"Don't look at me! I was at Children's House!" Katie said defensively.

"Katie saved the day by coming home when she did," Aunt Rainie interjected. "I guess Mel must have left a pot burning on the stove," she added in a small voice. Mel always left the pot he was using burning on the stove. Normally, someone was home to smell it burning and shut it off. Today, no one had been home but Mel.

Uncle Jeff's weathered face reddened to an alarming crimson. "Wait until I get hold of that lazy idiot!" he growled. Suddenly, he started to cough hard. He bent forward, clutching his chest as the coughing fit grabbed hold of him.

"Jeff!" Aunt Rainie cried in concern. "Jeff, just calm down. Lean on me now."

Uncle Jeff's steely blue eyes watered as he continued coughing. "It's the smoke in the air," Katie suggested to Aunt Rainie, worried by the ferocity of the coughing. "Maybe he should stand back from the smoke."

Aunt Rainie shook her head. "This has been happening for years. It's worse when he's upset." She guided him several paces back, away from the house.

Uncle Jeff's coughing subsided, and he stood, still bent forward, breathing heavily. Katie glanced over at Dizzy and smiled. Nagle, her small, fuzzy gray-and-white cat, had come from wherever he was hiding and now licked Dizzy kindly. Still weak, Dizzy gazed back at Nagle sweetly. Aunt Rainie's fat tabby, Myrtle, Nagle's mother, also appeared but hung back warily, viewing the excitement with suspicion.

"Don't worry, Jeff," Aunt Rainie said, her arms around her husband. "The house insurance will pay for the repairs. I always hated that ugly kitchen anyway. Aren't you glad I insisted we kept that policy up? You thought we'd never need it, but now look at this."

House insurance, that's right! Katie thought. All she knew about house insurance was that if you paid the insurance company money, then, if some sort of disaster happened, you'd have the money you needed to repair the damage. "So everything's going to be okay," Katie said, trying to be positive about this disaster. "You've got insurance."

Uncle Jeff raised his head and gazed at Aunt Rainie. Katie didn't like the sickened expression on his face.

Apparently, neither did Aunt Rainie, whose pale face turned a shade paler. "You did keep up the policy, didn't you, Jeff? I mean, you made the last payment, didn't you?"

Turning away from them, Uncle Jeff began coughing again, and this time the attack was even more violent than before.

4

The house reeked of smoke, reminding Katie of campfires. Only this smell didn't have that pleasant, woodsy aroma. It was sour and made her throat sore and her eyes water.

There was no escaping it, either. Downstairs, it was overpowering, almost nauseating. She'd come upstairs to get away from it, but even with her bedroom door shut, the smell drifted into her nose, making her sneeze.

At least it wasn't too cold upstairs. Not freezing, like it was downstairs. Uncle Jeff had used a heavy-duty staple gun to put thick, bright blue plastic over the yawning, charred holes in the walls and the large opening where the kitchen wall had collapsed.

"Why don't we just go to a motel, Jeff?" Aunt Rainie had suggested after the volunteer firefighters packed up their equipment and left.

"Can't afford it," Uncle Jeff mumbled, without looking away from his stapling. "This tarp will keep out the wind for tonight."

"Come on, Jeff! It's freezing," Aunt Rainie pleaded, whining just a bit.

"We can't leave the house unattended. Anyone could waltz right in here and dance out with our stuff," Uncle Jeff insisted.

What stuff? Katie had thought as she stood behind Aunt Rainie, rolling her eyes at Uncle Jeff's stubbornness. Was he worried about losing the hideous painting of a big hairy moose standing beside a waterfall which hung on the wall going up the stairs? Did he think someone might *dance* out with the lumpy, threadbare velveteen couch? Or was he worried about the TV set, which had such blurry, bad reception that it made Katie feel like she must need glasses.

Uncle Jeff had stepped back from his work, eyeing it critically and squinting his steely blue-gray eyes. Creases formed in his deeply lined brow. Then he nodded. "Perfect," he pronounced, clearly pleased with the tarp. "It's a beauty."

That was Uncle Jeff's idea of beauty. A dirty blue plastic tarp. Katie had sighed as she and Aunt Rainie followed Uncle Jeff through the opening at the side of the tarp and into the charred house.

"My beautiful kitchen," Aunt Rainie wailed, looking at the soot-caked walls, blackened stove and refrigerator, and scorched linoleum floor.

Katie felt sorry about the kitchen. But it had never been *beautiful.*

Boy, did Aunt Rainie and Uncle Jeff have bad taste!

Katie thought about it now as she sat cross-legged on her bed in her warmest red flannel pajamas, looking around her room. The silver-foil wallpaper had pictures of fat cherubs on it. Who in their right mind would pick out wallpaper like that? Her mother certainly wouldn't have. Their old apartment, back in the city, had been beautiful. Not because they'd been fabulously wealthy—they weren't—but because her parents knew how to put things together. All the rich colors looked good next to one another. The furniture was simple but nice.

Aunt Rainie and Uncle Jeff couldn't help it that they didn't have a lot of money, but did they have to buy such ugly stuff with the little they had? The things they bought —from Aunt Rainie's blindingly bright clothes to Uncle Jeff's hideous paintings—completely mystified Katie.

With a thud, the furnace kicked on, rattling the pipes. *Good*, Katie thought, pulling her comforter over her shoulders and wrapping herself in it. Things would warm up for a few minutes before all the warmth quickly seeped away under Uncle Jeff's *perfect* tarp.

Lucky Mel, she thought as she warmed the tip of her cold nose with her hand. He was someplace warm right now. He'd been too chicken to even come home. He must have figured out that the fire could be traced to him. She wondered how he'd even found out about the fire. But, then, Pine Ridge was a small town. News traveled fast.

There was a knock on her bedroom door. "Come in," Katie called.

Aunt Rainie appeared, dressed in a fuzzy orange robe with a long, metallic electric heater in her hand. "Here, honey," she said as she bent to the baseboard to plug the heater cord into an outlet. "Please remember to unplug this before going to sleep. The ancient wiring in these old walls isn't reliable. The heaters pull a lot of current and a wire could melt. We don't want another fire, lord knows. That's all we would need."

"I'll remember," Katie assured her as the heater came alive with an orangy-yellow glow behind its metal grate.

Aunt Rainie glanced at Dizzy, who was asleep, curled in the corner of Katie's room. Nagle also slept, in a ball by Dizzy's side. "Well, would you look at those two," she said with a soft chuckle. "Ain't that sweet?"

When Aunt Rainie left, Katie took two notebooks from the space between her mattress and box spring. A black-and-white marbled book was her journal, where she recorded her most private, inner thoughts; a red spiral notebook was for her short stories.

Katie planned to be a professional writer when she was older. Almost everything that happened made her think of a short story. She was always anxious to write the story down while it was fresh in her head.

Looking at the two books, she decided she'd prefer to begin a short story that had been slowly forming in her head ever since the fire that afternoon. Picking up the pen she kept clipped to the red book, she uncapped it and began to write.

THE FIRE
By Katie Nelson

Gigantic orange flames licked the sky as Melinda walked toward the towering, yet decrepit, lopsided house. At once, she knew her house would be engulfed in fire if she didn't do something. With the speed of a professional track star, she ran for the garden hose. She turned it on full blast, aiming it at the inferno.

Katie stopped a moment to savor the word *inferno.* She was always privately proud of herself when she came up with a good word like that. *Decrepit* was a good one, too. To her, finding great words was proof that she really had what it took to be an author. From time to time she doubted her ability, so these little proofs were encouraging.

The inferno abated.

Abated. Another great word. She was really on a writing roll.

Watching the abating inferno, Melinda noticed something black darting through the billowing black smoke. It was Goofy, the savage, jet-black half dog, half wolf owned by her drooling, dimwitted cousin, Marvin. Without a thought for her own safety, Melinda leaped into the smoke to save Goofy. Although Marvin owned Goofy, it was Melinda who had tamed and befriended the wild animal. Now she had to save her beloved companion, no matter what the cost.

All right. So it hadn't happened like that. This was

fiction. She didn't have to stick to the absolute truth. It made a much more interesting story the way she was telling it.

After several more paragraphs in which Katie related how Melinda staggered through the burning house with Goofy, she wound up with them trapped in the living room unable to find a way out.

"Now what?" she mumbled absently, staring at the cracked ceiling. She was stumped. How would she get them out of the blazing living room?

Getting out of bed, she started pacing thoughtfully. Dizzy opened one sleepy eye, studied her a moment, then returned to sleep.

Since her story was stalled, she decided to go brush her teeth and wash up for bed. Maybe an idea would come to her while she brushed. Opening her bedroom door brought a blast of frigid air from the hallway.

Wow, she thought. The electric heater had really done a good job heating up her room. It was freezing in the hall.

Clutching the collar of her pajama top to warm her neck, she scurried down the cold hall, barefoot, hurrying toward the bathroom at the end. On the way, she passed Aunt Rainie and Uncle Jeff's room. She could tell they were awake from the light shining under their door.

With her hand on the bathroom doorknob, about to turn it, Katie stopped abruptly. Aunt Rainie's voice had risen to an irritated, loud pitch, which Katie had never heard before.

"I still can't believe you didn't pay the insurance, Jeff!" she scolded.

Uncle Jeff said something, but Katie couldn't hear it.

Curious, she walked closer to the door. It would be fun to hear Uncle Jeff getting scolded. He was the one who usually did the complaining. And Aunt Rainie always gave in to him like he was the boss. Katie had never heard her aunt yell at her uncle. Not once.

"I told you to send in that payment. I told you we needed insurance," Aunt Rainie continued, clearly much more upset than she'd let Katie see earlier. "Now what are we going to do for a kitchen? How am I supposed to cook?"

"Heck, you hate to cook," Uncle Jeff mumbled.

"That is not the point!" Aunt Rainie shouted. "Hate it or love it, I have to do it! We can't live without a kitchen."

"Now don't go all crazy on me, Lorraine Marie Stopplemeyer," Uncle Jeff said. It sounded like he was moving around the room now. "I'll get you a kitchen."

"With what money, I'd like to know?" Aunt Rainie challenged. "It's not like we have a savings account, now, is it?"

"That is not my fault!" Uncle Jeff said firmly. "I was not the one who volunteered to take in the child of a relative we didn't even know all that well, was I?"

Katie froze. He was talking about her!

"What in heaven's name does Katie have to do with this?" Aunt Rainie shot back.

Katie leaned in closer to the door. What would he possibly reply? What *did* she have to do with it?

"Our girls are grown and married. And that idiot Mel is on his way out," Uncle Jeff continued truculently.

"Don't call Mel an idiot," Aunt Rainie clucked.

"Why not? He *is* an idiot! He acts like one most of the

time, anyway. It's true, even though he is my own son! Face it! He nearly burned the whole house down, Rainie!" Uncle Jeff insisted.

Katie nodded. That was true. Mel was definitely a self-centered idiot. She enjoyed hearing Uncle Jeff say so. But where did she come in? Did he think she was an idiot, too?

"Here's the problem with Katie," Uncle Jeff said.

Katie sucked her breath in, waiting to hear. What exactly did he think the problem with her was?

5

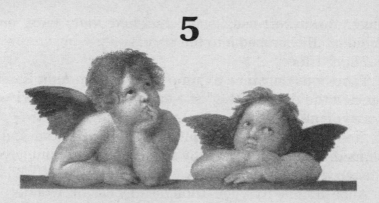

Katie leaned so close to the door that her ear brushed against the smooth wood.

"The problem is she costs money."

Aunt Rainie gasped. "How can you say that about our Katie? To begrudge her the money she—"

"Calm down, Rainie," Uncle Jeff interrupted. "All I'm saying is that I thought we'd be free and clear of supporting children by now. I didn't expect to have another child to look after at this stage of things. I hadn't figured it into our finances. So when Katie came along, I had to find more money, somehow. She's too young to earn her own keep, so someone has to pay her way. I thought that if I cut out the home insurance payment— which I never thought we'd need—it would be money we could use toward keeping Katie in clothing and books and whatever you're always spending money on her for."

Always spending money on me! Katie's mind screamed with outrage and her jaw dropped. In her anger and surprise, she clenched her fists and accidentally bumped into the door.

Thud! Uh-oh.

There was only time to jump away before Aunt Rainie opened the door. "Katie," she said, obviously surprised. "Are you all right? I heard a bump."

"Yes . . . I—I was heading for the bathroom and I slipped. I—I hit the door by mistake," she stammered, flustered and red-faced.

Aunt Rainie frowned thoughtfully, as if wondering whether Katie was telling the truth. "Are you all right, dear?"

"Yes. Fine," Katie said, backing up toward her room.

"I thought you were going to the bathroom." Aunt Rainie eyed Katie quizzically.

"I don't need to anymore," Katie replied quickly, wanting only to disappear. "I'm fine. Really."

Aunt Rainie nodded. "All right. If you're sure."

"Sure," Katie confirmed.

"Good night, then, sweetheart."

"'Night."

The moment Aunt Rainie's door closed, Katie ran to the safety of her bedroom. Shutting the door firmly behind her, she stood with her back against it. As her embarrassment at almost being caught eavesdropping faded, her indignation returned full-force.

What nerve! She was always so careful not to be a burden. She'd never asked them for anything she didn't absolutely need, nothing extra.

Nothing!

She couldn't help it if she needed clothing, school

supplies, and food. Didn't she work at the Pine Manor Horse Ranch during the summer to earn extra money? She tried to be so aware of their money problems, not like a lot of other kids she knew who never thought about their parents' finances.

Dizzy lifted his head and watched as she began pacing back and forth across the room.

How dare he say this was my fault? she ranted to herself, her heart pounding with hurt and outrage. Uncle Jeff was the one who didn't make the insurance payment. If it hadn't been for her, the house would have burned to the ground. But did he praise her for getting help so quickly? Did he say thank goodness Katie came home when she did?

No!

He just complained because he had to pay for her existence. It wasn't like he was giving her a life of luxury here in this drafty old house, either. She'd been a pretty good sport about it—a great sport!

She tried to make the best of the fact that she had a lot less than when her parents were alive. A *lot* less. He had no idea how little she complained, how she tried to cooperate. He just resented the *cost* of her.

"Sorry I'm so expensive, you cheapskate!" she spoke aloud. "The minute I turn eighteen, I'm out of here. You won't have to *pay* for me ever again!"

Her lip quivered. Uncle Jeff was so unfair! It just wasn't right!

Lately, she thought Uncle Jeff had stopped thinking of her as just this annoying drain on his wallet. In the beginning, when she'd first arrived, she'd often heard him make little complaining remarks about how much Katie cost. But recently, he'd stopped. He didn't seem to mind anymore. At least that's what she'd thought. She'd even been foolish enough to think he'd become fond of her in his own grouchy way.

Ha! What a laugh that was! Obviously, she'd been wrong.

A tear slid down her cheek. Briskly wiping it away, Katie bit down to steady her quivering lip. She hated these wounded feelings. She refused to feel hurt and unloved and alone. To feel pitiful.

It was unbearable!

It made her stomach hurt and her mouth dry. Her parents' death had caused her enough hurt to last her a lifetime. She didn't want to let hurt in, to feel its gut-twisting pain, anymore.

It was better to hold on to the outraged, insulted, proud side of herself. To be strong and angry—and right! It was definitely more comfortable. Pushing her jaw forward in an expression of stubborn determination, she focused herself on those feelings.

She scowled at the plump cherubs on her wall, smiling down at her with their fixed, benevolent smiles. What good were they? What she needed now were real angels. Angels who could airlift her out of this cold, smoky dump and take her somewhere far away, somewhere where she'd be appreciated and loved. They'd take her to a place where she could breathe freely without a miserable old man calculating the cost of the oxygen.

That wasn't going to happen, though. No angels were

coming for her. She knew it. It wasn't how angels worked.

"I know what I need," Katie whispered as an idea blossomed inside her. "My own money. Then Uncle Jeff couldn't complain about me."

With money, she'd eat out all the time, buy her own clothing, her own notebooks, her own everything. They'd hardly know she was there. She'd come home only at night, to sleep, and she could even pay rent to her aunt and uncle.

Rent! What a great idea! That would shut Uncle Jeff up once and for all. Even Mel—at twenty—didn't pay rent. And he spent more time in the house than anyone else.

Closing her eyes, she lifted her chin reverently to the ceiling. "Please, guardian angel," Katie whispered. "If you're around and you can hear me, I need money. As much as you can spare. Don't get the wrong idea. It's not that I'm greedy or anything. I need it so I don't have to bug my aunt and uncle anymore. That's a pretty decent reason, don't you think?" She paused a moment, deciding if she'd said everything she needed to say. "That's all. Thanks."

Feeling better—as though she'd taken a positive step toward solving her problem—Katie went back to her notebook on the bed. Somehow, in the middle of all her anger and upset, she'd come up with an answer to her story problem. Picking up her pen, she continued the story where she'd left off.

Melinda looked around frantically as the

horrifically ugly wallpaper melted off the walls. Flames shot in through the doorway. A line of flame burned up the carpet, revealing a trap door that had been hidden underneath the carpet. Putting Goofy down, she yanked on the door. "Come on, Goofy, it's our only way out," she said. But, when she opened the door, something bright shone up at her. "Gold," she cried. "Tons of it!"

But if there's gold blocking the way, that still doesn't get them out of the room, Katie considered. She yawned, suddenly tired. There had to be a solution to Melinda's problem. Maybe, after she scooped out the gold, Melinda would find a tunnel under the gold. Melinda and Goofy would escape through the tunnel, dragging the gold behind them.

Yes. That's what would happen, but she'd write it later. Right now she was too tired. She unplugged the heater, then jumped back into bed, cuddling down in her comforter while it was still warm.

Dizzy stood and then jumped onto the end of her bed. He'd never slept on her bed before. Katie wondered if the fire had made him feel scared.

Nagle scrambled up onto the bed, too. It was a little crowded, but the animals would keep her cozy once the warmth of the heater faded. Falling asleep quickly, Katie dreamed she was walking over mountains made of gold coins. Her heel started to slide on the coins, and soon she was tumbling down the hill of money, totally out of control.

Her eyes snapped open. *Whew! Good thing it was just a dream.*

The room was dark. The animals still slumbered on her bed. The tip of her nose was freezing. The cold air reeked of smoke.

Katie ducked under the comforter, burying her nose in her pillow. Tomorrow she would find a way to get that money.

6

The next day, after school, Katie took the school bus home with Christina and Ashley. "I still can't believe Christina told you to go home and when you got there your house was on fire," said petite Ashley, shaking her head in wonder. She leaned forward on the seat she shared with Christina and pushed back her wild mane of red curls, which fell past her shoulders. "I mean, I believe it. But it's so . . . so . . . awesome."

Katie leaned over the back of the seat, facing her friends. "It is pretty amazing," she conceded. "What does it feel like, Christina? When you get those *feelings*, what's it like? Do you hear a voice?"

"Not always, but this time, yes," Christina said. "This time I heard a soft voice say, 'Katie needs to go home,' as if someone were actually whispering in my ear."

Ashley looked from Katie to Christina, and her green eyes were wide. "An angel?" she whispered.

The girls looked at one another. "Maybe," Christina said quietly.

The bus slowed near a red barn bearing the large Pine Manor Horse Ranch sign. It was the ranch Ashley's family owned and worked. Christina's mother, Alice, worked there, too, as a riding instructor, trail leader, and ranch hand. Christina and Alice lived in their own cozy, rustic cabin on the ranch grounds.

The girls got off the bus and headed down a long dirt roadway. Katie tugged down on the brim of her navy blue baseball cap. Christina wrapped her long purple wool cape more tightly around her. Ashley shivered and yanked on the waist-length hem of her neat, trim, nubby green wool jacket.

On their left, split-rail fences marked the perimeters of the ranch's vast, softly rolling fields. Horses silently grazed, their long tails swishing the air, some of them standing in clusters, others alone.

To their right the majestic, ancient pines of the Pine Manor woods towered into the gray, cloudy sky. In its mysterious depths stood the Angels Crossing Bridge.

"Feel like going to the bridge?" Katie suggested, keeping her voice casual yet suddenly wanting very much to go.

"Why?" Ashley asked.

"We haven't been in a while. I was wondering if the angels were still there, even though it's getting cold."

"Cold doesn't matter to angels," Christina said. "Do you want to go because of the fire? I mean, because you're upset about the fire."

"In a way," Katie replied. Her friends knew her so well.

"All right," Ashley agreed. "Let's go. It's good to go to the bridge after something upsetting happens. It always makes me feel better. We just have to wait for Molly. Her dad is driving her over."

"Okay, good," Katie said. She didn't feel like talking about her other reason for wanting to go. Besides the comfort of being at the bridge after something scary, she wanted to go to make a request.

If the angels were there, she'd ask them for money in person, in case they hadn't heard her last night. At the bridge, she might see them. Then she'd know they'd heard her. Crossing her fingers, she hoped they'd be there.

A carpet of fallen pine needles muffled the sound of their footfalls as the girls made their way through the woods. A thin girl, whose waist-length, white-blond hair trailed down the back of her suede coat, walked slightly ahead of the others, chatting excitedly.

"Gosh, I wish I'd been there," said Molly Morgan, her sea-colored blue-green eyes dancing. "This would have come in super handy." She patted the small brown leather bag she wore over her shoulder. The case carried her cellular phone. "I could have called the fire department right on the spot. I've been dying for an emergency to come along so that I could really make this phone useful. If only I'd been there."

"Is that why you carry that phone everywhere?" Ashley asked.

"Sure. You never know," Molly replied dramatically.

"Well, it didn't matter," Katie told her. "I flagged down a police officer. And guess what. I'm pretty sure it was an—"

"An Officer Winger?" Christina jumped in.

Katie nodded.

"Wow!" the three girls intoned together, impressed.

"That's two times an angel might have helped you," Ashley noted. "One spoke to Christina. The other one was a Winger. Cool."

"The angels are thinking about you, Katie. That's for sure," Christina added.

"You really think so?" Katie asked hopefully. The idea made her happy and hopeful. Maybe she was on a winning streak when it came to angels. If so, could her money be far away? "How long have we been walking?" she asked, anxious to get to the bridge.

Molly checked her delicate silver watch. "Oh, no! My watch stopped. My good watch."

"You don't have anything that's *not* good," Katie said. Molly's wealthy parents gave her the best of everything.

"But this is my grandmother's watch. And it's broken."

"Maybe not. My watch stopped, too," Ashley said, looking at her plastic neon-colored watch. "How strange."

"Are we getting close to the bridge?" Christina asked. Katie understood what she meant. Was the bridge affecting their watches? Did it affect time itself?

The girls looked at one another. "I don't know if I've ever checked my watch before when we were in the woods," Ashley admitted.

"Me neither," Molly agreed. "But remember how my phone wouldn't work on the bridge? I wonder if the bridge throws out some kind of force field."

The girls nodded at one another. A force field. Katie let

the idea settle in. Was there some way to actually register the energy coming off the bridge? She liked the idea of being able to scientifically prove the mystical. On a public television program on physics, she'd heard about the vibration of matter. Things vibrated at different speeds. If something vibrated really fast—like a hummingbird's wings—after a certain speed you couldn't see it anymore. Maybe that explained angels. They were there, but vibrating so fast that you could see them only when they chose to slow down.

Nice theory, but she wanted proof. Photos. Some kind of Geiger counter that would register angel energy.

Yet proof kept slipping out of her hands the moment she thought she had it. She once had a photo of an angel, but then the angel mysteriously disappeared from the photo. There was the fact that Molly's phone didn't work on the bridge. And here was the business of the watches stopping.

But did it prove anything for certain? Did it? Not absolutely positively.

The only proof Katie had, she got through her eyes—and her insides. Deep within herself, she believed that when she saw the angels, they were real. She wasn't prone to "seeing" things. Never before had she ever thought she saw something that wasn't absolutely there. So Katie had no reason to doubt herself.

And she didn't. Not anymore. But, still . . . she longed for something that made this mystical, mysterious, awesome occurrence more understandable. Where did angels live? How did they work? How did they know the things they knew, and what gave them their power?

"What are you thinking?" Christina asked, breaking through Katie's musings.

"About angels," she replied. "About why the watches stopped, and Molly's phone."

At Katie's words, Molly took her phone from its leather pouch. She turned it on and held it to her ear. "No dial tone," she reported.

"We're close to the bridge," Ashley said.

"I wonder, if we brought a hundred people with watches and cellular phones here, and they all conked out, would it be positive proof that angels exist?" Katie pondered.

"But we don't want a hundred people here in our woods," Christina said, looking worried. "It would ruin the woods, and who knows what the angels would do."

"But just say we brought people here. It would be a big deal. It would be proof!"

"You know what I think?" Ashley offered. "I think the angels and the bridge and everything would simply disappear if we did that."

"I agree," Christina said.

Katie nodded. Maybe so. And her proof might slip away just as the angel in the photo had disappeared.

They continued walking through the ever more shadowy woods. After ten minutes or so (without working watches it was nearly impossible to tell, and in the woods it was easy to lose track of time), they came to a quick, babbling stream, running in a twisted path.

The stream would lead them to the bridge. They knew this because they'd followed it before. As they walked alongside it, Katie's feeling of excitement grew. Soon she'd be able to ask for wealth, in person.

She hoped so, anyway.

The angels weren't always there. *Be there today*, she said silently.

Finally the stream disappeared into the side of a wooded hill. It took less than five minutes to climb to the top. "There it is," Ashley murmured in awe. They all stared down at the covered wooden bridge at the base of the hill. It spanned a wide and rushing creek whose water sprayed, foamed, and danced over boulders, and then cascaded down a series of small waterfalls. The bridge's sides were open, exposing wooden supports that held up the roof.

Katie squinted hard at the bridge, holding her hand over her eyes like a visor. A break in the trees let in bright, white sunlight, which, after coming out of the dark woods, was nearly blinding. "I don't see anyone," she said quietly, more to herself than to her friends.

Wordlessly, they made their way down the hill toward the bridge. As she stepped onto its wooden floorboards, Katie shivered. A cold wind was rushing down the creek, blasting across the bridge. "Hello!" Katie called. "Anybody here?"

The wind whistled.

And then Molly's phone began to ring.

7

With wide eyes and opened mouths, the girls looked at one another. "I—I thought the phone didn't work on the bridge," Ashley stammered.

The phone continued ringing. "Answer it," Christina said, nodding at the phone.

Nervously, Molly took the phone from its pouch. Her hand trembled slightly as she clicked the phone on. "Hello?" she said in a small, shaking voice.

Suddenly a voice filled the cavernous bridge, as if Molly's phone were a speakerphone, broadcasting the voice of the person on the other end. "Hello, girls." It was a man's voice, deep and warm. Katie recognized it instantly and smiled.

"Ned!" she cried. Ned, Norma, and Edwina were the three angels who lived on this bridge.

"How is everything today?" he asked.

In hesitant, stammering voices, the girls replied. "F-f-fine."

"O-okay."

"N-not bad."

"I need to talk to you," Katie blurted.

"I know. Sorry we can't be there right now," he said, his voice filling the bridge.

"Where are you?" Christina asked in a friendly voice, the first to get over her nervousness.

"Ah . . . the moon, actually."

"What?" Katie cried.

"Yes, the moon. Wait a minute . . ." His voice grew more distant, as though he had turned away from the phone to ask a nearby person a question. "Ed, what year is it?"

"Nineteen sixty-eight. Or is it sixty-nine? I'm not sure," came a female reply, which they recognized as Edwina's sweet, slightly giddy voice. "I can never get this year business straight."

"It's the first moon walk, anyway," Ned said, coming in clearly again. "Very important stuff. These guys are brave but extremely nervous. Who wouldn't be?"

"Is there a problem?" Ashley asked.

"Not anymore," Ned replied. "One of their booster rockets conked out. But Norma and Edwina are fixing it now. They're under the rocket ship working. Norma is especially excellent with motors."

"With complex NASA engineering?" Katie questioned incredulously.

"Sure. No problem. Did you girls need something special?"

"Money!" Katie blurted.

A pause. The phone crackled.

"Money or wealth?" Ned asked.

What was the difference? Wealth sounded like a lot of money. Money could mean just a dollar-twenty-five. "Oh . . . uh . . . wealth. I need wealth," Katie amended. "Wealth for sure."

The line buzzed and crackled so loudly that the girls cringed and covered their ears. When the noise faded, Ned's voice again filled the bridge. "Sorry. I can barely hear you. There seems to be some interference. Meteor storm, I think. Would you repeat what you just said?"

"Wealth! I don't want to ask my aunt and uncle for any more money, so I need wealth!" Katie shouted, trying to talk over the static. "Any wealth you have to spare! I'll take it!"

"S . . . rry . . . C . . . n't . . . ear. Bye." Suddenly the line went dead. The rushing water of the creek was the only sound remaining.

"Call him back," Katie said urgently to Molly. "Quick."

"How do you call the moon?" Molly asked, staring at the phone, wide-eyed.

"I don't know. Press any button. Hit redial. Or what about star fifty-nine? Doesn't that dial back the last person who called you? Try that!"

Molly pressed buttons and listened. "Dead," she said. "The line's gone totally dead."

Katie slapped one of the bridge's wooden bracings in frustration. "I don't think he heard me. Do you think so? I don't know."

"He asked if you wanted money or wealth, so he heard you," Ashley said.

"Yeah, but I don't know if he heard my answer. What if I find a dollar blowing down the road? Does that mean my prayers have been answered? I need a lot more than that!"

She noticed Christina was staring at her with a wry, slightly disapproving expression. "What?" Katie snapped.

"You interrupted angels who were helping the first men on the moon to ask for money," she said, her voice stern and unbelieving.

"Wealth," Katie corrected coolly.

"Whatever!" Christina snapped, waving her hand as if to dismiss Katie's irrelevant reply. "How could you do that? How could you?"

"Well, he asked." Katie defended herself with an off-handed shrug. Turning her back on Christina, she walked to the side of the bridge and stared down at the churning white water below. Christina could be outraged if she liked, but Katie had come to the bridge to accomplish something important, and she wasn't about to let the chance to make her request pass her by. Still gazing down at the water, she cocked her head and twisted her mouth thoughtfully as a question occurred to her. "I wonder how Ned even knew we were here today," she murmured.

"Oh, they know everything," Molly said, coming to her side. "They sure seem to, anyway."

"I guess so," Katie agreed, nodding. "But did he hear me? Did he understand what I said to him?"

"Katie!" Christina cried in frustration. "Something completely awesome just happened. Angels spoke to us from the moon! The moon! Real angels on the moon! And you're worrying about getting extra cash. Why don't you just enter the state lottery and leave the angels out of it?"

"Why don't you mind your own business? You don't know anything about it!" Katie shot back angrily, whirling around to face Christina. "You're not me. Your mother doesn't count every nickel you cost her. You don't know how it feels. You have no idea! So why don't you be quiet about it!"

Christina's blue eyes widened with surprise as Katie turned away from her once again.

"Come on, let's not fight," Ashley intervened, stepping between Katie and Christina, "especially not here, on the bridge. This is . . . you know . . . a special place. Not a place to be fighting."

Katie clutched the rough wood on the bridge's railing and rocked slightly on the balls of her feet. Ashley was right, she thought grumpily. But Christina had been the one to open her big mouth about something that was none of her business. Still, she supposed, she herself often voiced her opinion even when no one asked for it. She was never exactly shy about doing that, so how could she blame Christina?

"Sorry," Christina muttered.

Katie swung around to face her. "Me too," she mumbled sullenly.

"Hey! Look!" Molly cried. They all stared as fat white flakes floated to the ground.

"How beautiful," Ashley sighed, leaning against the railing and stretching her hand out to catch a snowflake. "The first snow of the season."

"It's kind of early for snow. Do you think it's a sign?"

Katie asked hopefully. "A sign that Ned's going to answer my prayer?"

A frustrated sigh escaped Christina's lips, but Katie ignored it. Christina would never understand why the money was so important to her. There was no use trying to explain. She could never be in Katie's shoes. And it wasn't worth fighting about.

Together, they watched the snow fall. After several minutes, it started to stick to the ground and the rocks along the creek. "We'd better head back," Ashley suggested. "We don't want to get caught out here in a blizzard."

In silent agreement, the girls headed off the bridge. Once they were back under the pines, the snowfall lessened. Only a few flakes drifted through the dense pine covering overhead. But Katie could tell it had turned colder. And there was an eerie silence blanketing the woods. *Why?* she wondered. Then she realized it was the absence of animal sounds. No twigs snapped, no squirrels scrambled in the overhead trees. The birds didn't flit from branch to branch or call playfully to each other.

The animals had taken cover to get away from the coming storm. They now curled in underground burrows; nestled on branches, their feathers puffed for warmth; or huddled in the hollows of trees.

Realizing this made Katie quicken her pace. If the animals had scrambled for shelter, shouldn't they do the same?

Overhead, the trees swayed, their branches rubbing against one another. From time to time a huge wind would rock them hard.

The girls followed the winding stream back through the woods, quickly retracing their way back to the ranch. As she stepped across a very narrow section of stream, Katie stopped short.

Several yards away, a figure was coming toward them. A figure with wings spread wide.

8

Standing close together, the girls watched the figure come closer. It looked small and female, and moved unevenly, darting first this way, then that. Sometimes it disappeared behind a tree, then popped out again just when it seemed it was gone for good.

A sprinkling of snowflakes fell all around, drifting on the breeze. It made Katie feel like she was in one of those small shaker balls, a snowdome. The figure seemed to shimmer in the snow.

"An angel," Christina said with quiet awe.

"No," Ashley disagreed cautiously. "I don't think so."

"But it has wings," Molly said.

Katie peered hard at the figure. "No, not wings. That's a shawl blowing from her arms. A white shawl with beads or something on it."

Disappointment made a dry lump in her throat. For a moment, she'd actually thought it was an angel with a bag of money for her. She'd hoped the answer to her request could be that immediate.

But no.

The woman caught sight of them and let out a cry that sounded like recognition. "Ah!" she said, and threw out her arms. "I have been waiting for you."

"She's coming toward us," Molly noted, slightly panicked.

"Why would she be wandering out here in the woods like this?" Ashley wondered aloud. Almost no one came into the Pine Manor woods except trail riders on horse-back from the ranch.

"My friends! My friends!" the woman cried when she was about three yards away. "I am so glad you have come to help me." Her voice was thick with an accent. Katie guessed it might be a Russian accent.

As she got closer they could see her eyes, small, black, and deeply set in her round, finely lined face. The old woman's face made Katie think of the man in the moon, only in this case it would be the woman in the moon. Her glance darted over each of the girls, eagerly taking them in, and those lively eyes danced with a shining inner light. Moonlight.

Lunar light. Looney light.

She wore a long brown baggy dress and heavy work boots. Her angel-like aura came from a soft white woolen cap and a matching shawl. Both were covered with translucent, sliver-thin, opalescent sequins that jiggled and caught the light, making the woman sparkle.

"She needs help," Christina said, stepping forward past Katie. "Are you all right?" she asked.

At close range, they saw that the woman's face was smeared with dirt, her frazzled white hair unbrushed.

She's a homeless person, Katie thought, remembering the many homeless people she'd seen when she lived in the city. *And she's not right in the head.* Something in those burning, busy eyes suggested mental instability to Katie. She'd seen it before in people wandering the city streets, talking to themselves at full volume.

With a long step, she fell back behind the others, nervous about meeting this person.

But Christina, followed by Ashley, plunged forward to help the woman. Molly hung back beside Katie, fingering the strap of her phone pouch, thinking this might be the moment to make an emergency call—she was far enough from the bridge for the phone to work again.

"Are you lost?" Christina asked gently, bending toward the small woman. "You should get inside. It's snowing." She gestured around to indicate the falling snow. Katie rolled her eyes. Of course the woman could see the falling snow. Did Christina think she was blind or something?

Yet, amazingly, the woman looked at the snow as if noticing it for the first time. "Oh! Pretty! Yes! Snow. A good sign! A lucky sign!"

Stepping forward, Katie stared at the woman. Obviously she wasn't dangerous. In fact, she looked kind of sweet with her round face and small upturned nose. "Come on," she said to Molly as she stepped forward.

"You girls," the woman said as she fumbled in the pocket of her baggy dress. "You know these woods? Yes?" The woman held out a worn, dirty scrap of folded paper she'd found in her pocket. "You show me then this spot?" She nodded as she spoke. "You find this spot for Anna. Yes? Please."

Katie reached out for the fragile paper. Holding it gingerly, she looked down at words written in an angular, very slanted handwriting filled with extravagant flourishes and loops. An old-fashioned handwriting. She couldn't understand the words. They were in a language she didn't recognize.

Below the writing, three lines intersected, meeting at a point on one wavering horizontal line. "A map?" she asked the woman.

"Yes, a map. Treasure. Anna's treasure. We find. I will give you some."

Katie's heart pounded. This was it. Her wealth. The answer to her prayer.

"Where could this be?" she wondered aloud, staring at the yellowed sketch in her hand.

"It's getting colder," Ashley said to the woman. "You need something warmer to wear."

"No. I am warm. I must find my precious treasure. The time is running short for me. They will come for me soon, and I must have the treasure."

Katie glanced up from the mysterious sheet of paper. Yes. Crazy. This woman was definitely crazy. She thought someone was after her. She thought she had a treasure map.

But . . . who knew? Maybe it was true.

Ashley took hold of the old woman's arm. "Come home with me," she said with friendly firmness. "It's cold. You can't stay here."

The woman yanked away fiercely, her eyes blazing like those of a cornered animal. "No!" she shouted. "I won't go back without my treasure!"

"But . . . but . . ." Ashley stammered helplessly. "You can't stay here."

"Yes! Yes!" the woman insisted, backing away.

"We just want to . . ." Christina began, but she didn't get to finish. The elderly woman turned and fled into the woods, her shawl flying behind her.

"Wait!" Katie shouted after her. "I have your map!" She waved the map and began running after the woman. After several yards she stopped, looking in all directions. "Where'd she go?" she asked, turning back to her friends.

"She went behind those trees, and then I didn't see her again," Molly said. "She might have ducked behind those thick pines."

Katie stared down at the worn, yellowed map fluttering in her hand and wondered if it was, indeed, the answer to her prayers.

9

At the ranch, the girls raced up the steps of Ashley's neat, one-story house and bounded into the living room. "Mom!" Ashley called.

A petite woman with short, reddish hair came out of the kitchen drying her hands on a dish towel. "What? What is it?" she asked, her green eyes wide with alarm.

Ashley's tall, broad-shouldered father stepped out of his small office off the living room. "What's the matter?" he asked, his frown deepening the creases in his chiseled features.

"There's an old woman in the woods," Ashley said, then went on to tell her parents about Anna. "I think she might be a little crazy," she added. "I don't know if she has enough sense to come in out of this snow."

Mrs. Kingsley sighed thoughtfully. Then she went back into the kitchen and phoned the Pine Ridge police, asking if an old woman fitting Anna's description had been reported missing. "No one, you say," she murmured. "Well, can't you do something? She shouldn't be wandering by herself in the woods. Who knows when this snow will stop."

With a frustrated sigh, Mrs. Kingsley finally hung up.

"What did they say?" Christina asked.

"Not much," Ashley's mother replied. "The police officer on the other end of the line wasn't sure if the police had the right to go out looking for Anna. She hasn't committed a crime, and no one has filed a missing persons report on her," Mrs. Kingsley reported. "He said he'd talk to his sergeant and call back." She turned to Mr. Kingsley. "I had Marty Tyson on the phone."

Mr. Kingsley nodded. In a small town like Pine Ridge, everyone knew everyone else, and the Kingsleys had lived there all their lives.

Glancing out the window, Katie saw that the snow was still falling.

"Hank," Mrs. Kingsley said to her husband. "Would you go look for that woman? She could freeze to death out there."

"You're right. Sure," he replied. "I'll bring Jeremy and Jason with me," he added, referring to Ashley's seventeen-year-old twin brothers.

"I'd better help Alice get the rest of the horses in," Mrs. Kingsley said as she followed Ashley's father out of the kitchen.

The girls sat around the kitchen table. "I wonder who Anna is," Christina said, her chin resting in her hands.

"A wacky old lady looking for treasure," Molly answered simply.

"Do you think there really is treasure hidden out there?" Christina asked, furrowing her brow skeptically.

"There could be," Ashley said thoughtfully. "It's called the Pine Manor woods because there was once a big house back there in the woods. A manor house—a sort of mansion. The angel bridge is there because there was once a road running up to the house."

"That makes sense," Molly agreed. "Normally you don't see a bridge in the middle of a forest unless there was once a road there. What happened to the house?"

"It burned down," Ashley told her. "That was a long time ago, like around World War I or something, I think. My grandfather told me about it. He said that after the fire, they never rebuilt the house and the road stopped being used. Trees just grew over it until the road finally disappeared altogether."

"So someone who lived in that house could have hidden treasure in the woods," Christina said slowly. "But why would they?"

"Who knows," Molly said with a shrug. "People hide things for all sorts of strange reasons." She looked over to Katie. "You're quiet. What are you thinking?"

"Could Anna have been an angel?" Katie asked. She couldn't get over the coincidence that she'd asked for wealth and then Anna had appeared. By now she knew that angels sometimes worked in odd ways.

Christina, Ashley, and Molly looked at one another with questioning eyes. "I don't know," said Ashley. "I suppose anyone could be an angel. Do you think she was?"

"I don't know," Katie said, drumming her fingertips on the table. "I don't know."

* * *

The next day in school, Katie couldn't stop thinking about Anna. Mr. Kingsley, Jeremy, and Jason hadn't found her, although they'd searched for over an hour. The police called back to say they couldn't send out a search party, but they were calling police in nearby towns to see if anyone there knew who Anna might be.

Whenever she had a free moment, Katie took out the map and smoothed it on her desk. Something about those intersecting lines had to have some meaning. Where were those lines pointing? She scowled at the map, trying to force her mind to produce the answer.

After school, Katie went to a meeting for *The Writer*, the school newspaper for which she wrote stories and took photos. Arriving a few minutes early, she took her seat at a long table across from Darrin Tyson, a stocky boy with bright blue eyes and short, spiky blond hair, who wrote the sports column. "Hey, Nelson," he greeted her gruffly.

"Hi, Darrin," she said quickly. She had no desire to talk to him. He wasn't really a terrible guy, just a pain. He seemed to live just to annoy her, and given half a chance he would find a way to do it. Angling her back to him, she took out her map. She just couldn't stop looking at it. There was a secret in this map, and it would drive her crazy until she cracked its code.

"What's that?" Darrin demanded, craning his neck to see the map.

"Nothing," Katie said, folding the map and slipping it into her math textbook. "Nothing."

Darrin reached across the table. "Come on, Nelson, let me see what . . ."

"Great news," exclaimed short, perky Sally Overton, the student editor of the paper, as she bustled excitedly into the office. "You're not going to believe this!"

"What?" Katie asked eagerly, putting her hands protectively across her math book to keep Darrin away from the map.

Sally removed her glasses and cleaned them as she waited for three other kids to take their seats. "Listen to this," she said, replacing her glasses and smoothing her frizzy, shoulder-length brown hair. "The Parent-Teacher Association is sponsoring a trip to Washington, D.C., for the staff members of the paper to cover the annual Kids Count Too Conference!" She smiled and waited for them to respond.

"What the heck is that?" Darrin asked, unimpressed.

"Don't you watch TV?" Sally asked, shocked at his ignorance. "It's the big meeting of kids to discuss world issues. They're going to draft a kids' proposal to change the world."

"I've heard of it. Way to go!" Katie cheered as everyone else around her murmured excitedly. A trip to Washington! Katie longed to travel, and she'd never been to the capital. This was too exciting for words.

"The PTA is paying most of the expenses," Sally went on. "But we'll each have to pitch in a hundred dollars to help cover meals. I'm sure your parents won't care when they find out you're going to get an entire three days in D.C. for only a hundred dollars."

"That's cheap," said Rhonda Lynbrook, a pretty blond girl wearing thick mascara, who wrote a column about fashion.

Cheap? Katie thought, as her heart sank in disappointment. Of course, Rhonda could say that. Rhonda's parents obviously had a lot of money. Rhonda always looked like she'd stepped out of a fashion magazine.

But one hundred dollars wasn't cheap if you didn't have it.

Christina slipped breathlessly into the seat beside Katie. "I had to finish up this horoscope column at my locker," she whispered as she straightened the papers in front of her. "What's going on?"

"We're going to Washington," Katie whispered back glumly.

"Cool!" said Christina. Noticing Katie's dismal expression, she opened her mouth to ask about it but was interrupted by Sally.

"It's two weekends from now," Sally continued. "We have the long weekend because of the teachers' conferences. Is there anyone who can't go at that time?"

Slowly, Katie raised her hand.

"Katie, you have to go!" Sally cried. "Nobody else can take a decent picture."

"Hey, I resent that!" Darrin shouted. He took photos for his sports column.

"Face it, Darrin, your pictures could use work," Sally said bluntly. "They're always blurred."

"They're action shots," Darrin grumbled.

"Why can't you go, Katie?" Sally asked.

Katie felt herself blushing with embarrassment, which only made matters worse. "Um . . . I'm not sure if I can . . . uh . . . get the money," she mumbled.

"You can't?" Sally cried. "Are you sure?"

"Uh . . . well . . . you see . . . we just had a fire at my house and things are a little tight now."

"What a lame excuse," Rhonda whispered loudly to a girl named Candy Martin, who sat beside her.

Katie felt her blush deepen. "It's not an excuse," she said harshly. "It happens to be the truth."

"Sure. Whatever you say," Rhonda replied in a voice thick with sarcasm.

"What's your problem?" Katie challenged.

"Nothing," Rhonda yelped. "I could care less if you go or not."

Katie felt like pushing Rhonda right out of her seat. She'd never liked the girl, thinking she was phony and shallow. But why was she being so mean? Katie knew why. Rhonda and Ashley had both liked the same boy at one time. In the end, Rhonda wound up dating him. But even though she was the winner, Rhonda had never liked Ashley after that, and she extended her dislike to Ashley's friends.

"I know, Katie! We could take up a collection for you," Sally suggested enthusiastically. "If everyone donated ten dollars you could go."

Katie paled.

A collection! For her? How humiliating! She might be an orphan, but she didn't need charity. "No way!" Katie said, waving away the idea. "No collections. I'll get the money. Don't worry. I'll be there. I don't need any collections. Thanks but no thanks."

It was Sally's turn to blush. "I'm sorry. I didn't mean to embarrass you. I just thought that—"

"I'm not embarrassed," Katie cut her off sharply. "I'm

sure I'll be able to go if I just ask. Forget I said anything."

For the rest of the meeting, the staff talked about the lineup for their special Washington issue. Katie volunteered to take pictures of the staff in front of famous monuments, like the Lincoln Memorial and the Capitol building. She also agreed to cover the first day of the conference, take pictures, and report on it.

"Are you sure you'll be able to cover those stories?" Sally asked her. "If you can't go, it's okay. I didn't mean to—"

"I can do the stories," Katie assured her. "Absolutely."

After the meeting, Katie and Christina waited for Christina's mother to come pick them up. "I'd loan you the money, but I only have a hundred and ten dollars saved from our summer jobs. Don't you have any of that money left?"

"No," Katie replied, kicking at the melting remains of slushy, gray snow. "I used it because I hate to ask my aunt and uncle for anything like movie money or junk like that."

"Why not ask Molly?" Christina suggested. "You know she can afford it. I'm sure she wouldn't mind helping you out."

"That's not right," Katie disagreed as she jammed her hands in her coat pockets. "I don't want to mooch off her just because her parents are rich."

"But you wouldn't be mooching. You'd pay her back," Christina said.

"How?" Katie asked. "I won't have a job again until next spring, when school ends. That's too far away."

A brown pickup truck drove up the hill leading to the

school. "There's Mom," Christina said. "I wish I had the money to give you. Do you think your aunt and uncle can spare it?"

"Tightwad, cheapskate Uncle Jeff?" Katie hooted. "Not likely."

That night, the house was bitterly cold. The dank smell of smoke was still everywhere. The blue plastic tarp over the side of the kitchen where the wall had collapsed crackled and flapped as the wind tugged at it.

Wrapped in a blanket, Katie sat on the velveteen couch in the living room, watching an old black-and-white movie and eating one of the ham sandwiches Aunt Rainie had brought home for supper.

She wasn't really paying attention to the movie. Her mind was on getting the money for the trip to Washington. She'd come up with a plan she wanted to suggest to her aunt and uncle.

Her parents had left some money for her to be used for her education. She'd found out about it when Molly had taken Katie and her friends to her family's castle in Ireland. Aunt Rainie had dipped into the fund so Katie could afford the airfare. She justified it by saying that traveling was educational.

Well, wasn't this also educational? Katie had begun to feel confident that her aunt would agree to take some of the education money for this trip. It was only a hundred dollars, after all.

A loud crinkling of the tarp told her someone had come in from outside. It was Mel. Her tall, overweight cousin pushed his black bangs from his eyes and managed to look defensive and nervous at the same time. It was his first time home since the fire. "Hi," he said, looking around. "Are my parents here?"

"Upstairs," Katie told him.

Warily he glanced at the stairs. "They mad?"

"You could say that," Katie told him. "Probably not as mad as they were at first."

"It wasn't my fault, you know," Mel said.

Boy, he's scared, Katie thought with some satisfaction. Normally he wouldn't bother explaining anything to her. Mel was so self-centered. "Then how come you haven't come home?" Katie asked as she took another bite of her sandwich.

Mel scowled at her. "I've been busy."

"Okay," Katie said with a shrug.

"Besides, I know they'll blame me because I was the last one home. But I shut everything off before I left. I know I did. I mean, anyone could leave a burner on and not realize it, I guess. But I'm pretty sure, you know?"

Yeah, sure, Katie thought. Any time Mel cooked anything for himself, he left the pot to burn on the stove. The whole family knew that.

Aunt Rainie's voice floated down the stairs. "Mel? Is that you?"

Mel uttered a curse under his breath and looked like he wanted to make a run for it. Aunt Rainie came down the stairs. "Hi, hon," she said pleasantly. "Could you come upstairs, please? Dad and I need to talk to you."

Trapped, Mel hung his head and skulked upstairs.

Unexpectedly, Katie felt sorry for him. It wasn't as if he *meant* to burn the kitchen down, after all.

When the movie ended, Katie threw off the blanket and headed up to her room to do homework and then go to bed. On the second floor, she saw Mel storm out of his parents' bedroom and into his own room across the hall. *I guess that didn't go too well*, she surmised.

She jumped back startled as Uncle Jeff stepped out of his room. His face was an angry storm cloud. He came down the hall toward her, but his head was down and he only noticed her when he was almost next to her.

"Hi, Uncle Jeff," Katie said in a small voice.

"Hi," Uncle Jeff muttered, passing by.

Aunt Rainie was last out of the room. "Oh, Katie," she said, seeing her niece. Her face was tight with worry, but she relaxed it before speaking. "Is everything all right?"

"Yes," Katie replied. This didn't seem like the moment to ask Aunt Rainie for the Washington money. She wanted to, badly. *No . . . better to wait*, she decided.

"Did you do your homework, honey?"

"Uh, not yet, but I will. I was just about to."

"Good. I have to go discuss something with your uncle. Excuse me," Aunt Rainie said, hurrying down the hall and disappearing down the stairs.

Katie went into her room, where Dizzy and Nagle were sleeping together in a corner they had obviously claimed as their own. Dizzy lifted his head in a sleepy greeting, and Nagle stirred, awakened by his movement. Katie ran a hand along Dizzy's back and scratched Nagle between his ears. Then she looked for her school backpack.

"It's downstairs," she muttered. She'd left it on the couch.

Leaving her room, she headed back down the stairs

but stopped on the third step from the top. Her aunt and uncle spoke in hushed, inaudible, agitated voices. She wasn't sure she should intrude.

As she turned to go back up to her room, she heard Aunt Rainie sobbing loudly.

"Aw, come on, now, Rainie," Uncle Jeff said in a voice at once gruff yet tender. "Things aren't all that bad. I'll just take the money from her."

Katie froze. What money was he talking about? Her school money?

"It doesn't seem right," Aunt Rainie said through her tears. "That's special money. We shouldn't touch it."

Breathing in sharply, Katie hunched her shoulders in shocked outrage. It had to be her school money! What other money did they have? None! Uncle Jeff always made that all too perfectly clear.

Uncle Jeff laughed joylessly. "Right now we need it a lot more than she does. It was put away for the future. But the future's come a little sooner than we expected, that's all. Besides, she don't need it, and she'll never even know it's gone. I promise you that," he said.

Oh, yes, I do know it's gone, Katie thought bitterly. Not only was her uncle a cheapskate, he was a thief, too. He was taking her money, money from her parents. The money they'd so lovingly set aside for her in case anything ever happened to them.

It was too awful to be true. Yet it was true. She'd just heard it for herself.

Katie hurried to her room and bounced down hard onto her bed. Her aunt and uncle were monsters. She'd tried to see the good in them, tried to love them. But now she knew what they really were. Horrible, selfish thieves.

How could they do this to her? Especially Aunt Rainie! How could she agree to it? So what if she seemed kind? She was a monster, too, because she didn't stand up to Uncle Jeff.

Katie thought they'd started to love her. But they didn't! If they loved her, they would never steal from her.

She had to be free of them. "The map," she said quietly. "The map was sent to me for a reason."

Angels sent it so she could get away from her horrible aunt and uncle. That had to be it.

"And I'm going to find that treasure," she vowed.

The next day, Katie burned inside, dying to get back into the woods and find that gold. It was all she could think of all morning in school. But to her dismay, around lunch time, she remembered that she'd promised Christina she'd go over to the Pine Ridge Nursing Home with her. Christina wanted to scout out a good location for their show.

She couldn't let Christina down, not after she'd promised.

They took the bus to the home, which was separated from the Pine Ridge Hospital by a busy, two-lane highway. "I hope I never get old," Katie muttered as they entered the plain, square building. She didn't like the antiseptic smell of the place, or the dull landscape paintings on the brown walls.

A short, friendly nurse greeted them. "Are you the girls Ms. Baker told me were coming?" she asked with a smile.

"Yes," Christina replied.

"Hello. I'm Ms. McCrain, head nurse here. I think I have the perfect place for your show," she said, waving for them to follow her down the hall. She led them to a large, sunny room. It was more homey than the rest of the place. It had a blue carpet and tall windows with matching blue drapes. Comfortable chairs were scattered around, and Katie noticed folding chairs stacked along the wall. "This is our social room," Nurse McCrain explained.

"This looks great," Christina said, stepping into the room enthusiastically. "We can line the kids up in a sort of horseshoe. Can we move the chairs into a circle?"

"I don't see why not," Nurse McCrain agreed.

At that moment a very old woman wheeled herself into the room. "Hello, Clara." The head nurse greeted her. "Can I help you with something?"

Katie couldn't take her eyes off the woman. She was the oldest person she'd ever seen. She was tiny, and every inch of her seemed wrinkled. Her snowy hair was so wispy fine it revealed her smooth scalp underneath. Yet her eyes were alive with movement and light.

Nurse McCrain noticed Katie's expression. "Clara is one hundred and five." She spoke with admiration, as though Clara's age were an accomplishment to be proud of.

"Wow," was all Katie could think of to say.

"Old, isn't it?" Clara said with a wry smile.

"Do you know about the show?" Christina asked her.

"Yep. That's why I'm here. To see it," Clara said. "I wanted to get a good seat."

"It's not this weekend. It's next weekend," Nurse McCrain told her.

As she spoke, another nurse came into the room. "We need you in room seven, Ms. McCrain."

"Excuse me," said the nurse. "I'll be right back."

On her way out, Nurse McCrain passed a beautiful young woman with wavy brown hair, dressed in a soft, flower-patterned dress. The woman stood behind Clara, and the old woman smiled fondly up at her. "Another week, eh," she said. "I guess I'll have to hang on another week before I check out for good."

"Don't say that," Katie said. "Don't talk that way."

"Honeybun, I'm one hundred and five," Clara said, leaning forward in her wheelchair. "I'm going to die. There's no getting out of it. It's okay. I've had a long life, as you can see, and thankfully I haven't been really sick like a lot of my friends here. So I have nothing to kick about."

Katie nodded. What could she say? Clara was only telling the truth.

"Are you her daughter?" Katie asked the beautiful woman.

"No," the woman said. "Just a good friend."

"I'm looking forward to this show," Clara said. "Before I die, I want to see a show with children, because children are the most beautiful, precious things on earth."

"You're going to love it, then," Christina assured her. "The kids are working so hard, and they're so excited about it."

Clara nodded and her eyes grew heavy. Settling back in her chair, she closed her eyes and her body went limp.

Katie tensed. Had Clara died right before her eyes? "She's not . . . she isn't . . . you know?" she asked the beautiful woman.

"Just sleeping," the woman said as she took a throw blanket from the back of Clara's wheelchair and covered Clara with it.

"That's a relief," Katie said. "She's lucky to have such a good friend as you to take care of her."

"She's a good woman," Clara's companion said with a fond smile. Smoothly, she wheeled the sleeping woman out of the room.

"See now how important this show is?" Christina asked. "People like Clara will enjoy it so much. It will mean so much to them."

"Yeah, I guess so," Katie agreed absently. She was distracted, watching the elderly people who'd begun coming into the room. They reminded Katie of Anna. What was she doing now? Was she frantic, wondering when and if Katie would return the map to her? Or did she know it by heart already? Maybe she didn't need the map. Perhaps she'd found her treasure and left the woods already.

"Do you need help with the show tomorrow?" Katie asked Christina.

"Not tomorrow. Why?"

"Because I'm going back into the woods to try to find that old woman we met," Katie explained. "I'm going to help her find that treasure."

"That's really nice of you," Christina commented, impressed.

"I'm not doing it to be nice," Katie said candidly.

"I'm doing it because she said she'd share it."

"Okay," Christina said, absorbing this information. "But do you really think there is a treasure?"

"For some reason, I'm positive there is," Katie told her. "I think the angels sent Anna to me to answer my request for wealth."

10

"This is crazy," Ashley said the next day after school as she and Katie stood behind the stable, staring into the woods. Molly and Christina were busy studying for a test, but Katie had convinced Ashley to join her in her search for Anna. Now Ashley was having second thoughts.

"We'll never find Anna," Ashley said, shaking her head. "My father and brothers looked everywhere."

"I have to find her," Katie insisted stubbornly. "I have to get away from the thieves. My aunt and uncle. Mr. and Mrs. Thief."

"Are you sure you heard them right?" Ashley questioned.

Katie shook her head confidently. "This morning—just to be sure—I asked Aunt Rainie if I could have some of my money for the Washington trip. Guess what she said."

"What?"

"She said no. She said, 'I'm sorry, dear, but I don't want to dip into the money for everything. It could get to be a bad habit.'" Katie smiled scornfully. "Bad habit my foot.

Don't you think that proves they're taking my college money?"

"Well," Ashley said uncertainly, "not really."

"Of course it does! Why would they pay for a trip to Ireland but not a school trip to Washington? It doesn't make sense. They're taking the money, all right. You wait and see. Uncle Jeff is going to suddenly come up with some money for a new kitchen right out of the clear blue sky. Just wait."

Ashley sighed miserably. "All right. Let's look for Anna."

The girls entered the woods, which were shadowed with dying late-afternoon light. "Anna!" Katie shouted. "Anna! Where are you?"

Only the wind whistling through the trees answered.

"I just thought of something," Katie said. "Anna might not come out if she sees you. It might scare her if there are two of us. Remember how she ran the other day? She thought you and Christina were going to force her to go with you. You'd better go back."

"That's true, but . . . are you sure?" Ashley asked.

"Yes. I bet she'll keep hiding if she sees you. But she might come out if she sees me, because I have her map. She'll want it back."

"Don't stay too long," Ashley warned. "You don't want to get lost out here in the dark."

"That's for sure," Katie agreed. "I'll come back before too long."

With a wave, Ashley turned and walked back to the ranch. Katie moved steadily through the woods, calling the old woman's name. Her voice echoed, cracking open the silence as she passed the small stream.

In the distance, Katie began to hear the rushing water of the creek. She climbed the hill and looked down at the Angels Crossing Bridge.

The old woman stood on the bridge, her arms spread wide, her shawl making wings.

Katie's blood pumped with new hope and excitement as she ran down the hill.

Anna remained standing with her arms wide and her face raised to the ceiling until Katie reached the bridge. At the sound of her footfall on the wooden planks, Anna lowered her gaze and spied Katie. "Ah, my friend. I was certain you would come back."

"You were?" Katie asked, surprised.

"Yes. And here you are. Very good. Very good. You have brought back my map?"

Katie took the map from her pocket and held it out. The woman's wrinkled face shone with joy as she took it. "You are the answer to my prayers."

"I thought you were the answer to *my* prayers," Katie said sheepishly.

"Perhaps we were sent to one another," Anna said. "I come to this place when I need help, because there is something special here."

"You know about the bridge?" Katie's eyes were wide with amazement.

"Yes. Of course." She came close to Katie and took hold of her wrist with a surprisingly strong grasp. "When I was a girl, I saw *angels* on this bridge. With my own eyes! Angels! You believe?"

"Yes, yes," Katie said. "I do believe you."

Anna let go of Katie's wrist and nodded knowingly.

"When I am a girl, I live in the great house with my parents. My father is a count, my mother a countess. But they die in terrible fire. Now I reclaim the treasure my father left. I come back to take what is mine."

As Anna spoke, Katie felt her pulse quicken excitedly. Anna's story sounded so possible. She knew there was a manor house here and that it had been destroyed by a fire.

Anna knew that the bridge was a special place, too. Other people might think that sounded strange, but Katie knew it was true.

Since Anna wasn't crazy about those things, perhaps she wasn't crazy at all. Maybe she was an unusual person, but not crazy. The treasure might be very real. "What kind of treasure is it?" Katie asked, breathless with excitement. "Is it money? Jewelry?"

"Angels," Anna replied, her voice an awestruck whisper—soft and filled with reverence.

"Angels?" Katie asked.

"The most beautiful, golden angels you have ever seen."

Angels of pure gold! Imagine! Katie easily envisioned them glistening, heaped on top of one another in some ancient trunk. Bars of shining gold, fashioned into the shapes of angels. What could be more fitting?

"You help me find and I share them with you, my friend," Anna said.

Yes! Katie thought jubilantly. This was really happening. The angels might have been on the moon, but they had heard her. They'd sent golden angels to her.

Now all she had to do was find them.

11

Katie stamped her feet on the cold, hard ground to warm them. "We should go back," she told Anna. "It's getting dark."

They'd been searching in the woods for hours: fumbling in the hollows of fallen trees; overturning heavy boulders that might block secret openings in the ground below; wrestling with the dead, scratchy brown branches of huge fallen pines—just in case they concealed a trunk of golden angels.

So far, they'd turned up nothing.

And now the unearthly golden light of the sunset filtered down through the shadowy woods. No matter how badly she longed for those golden angels, Katie feared being stuck in the woods after dark. She'd been lost in the woods before, and it was an awful, terrifying experience she didn't want to repeat. "We can try again tomorrow," Katie coaxed Anna.

"No! No!" Anna said, letting her hand fly up in the air as if to push away the very idea of leaving. "We must look at the map. The map tells us."

"But we don't understand the map," Katie reminded her. Although Anna could read the Russian words, she didn't understand their meaning. Her small, quick, birdlike eyes bored into the map as she read them again, translating for Katie.

"Where the lines meet, three together, there have I hidden my little girl's treasure."

"Why did your father hide it?" Katie asked.

"It was a game. Every year, before Christmas, he would hide the chest. Then he would give a map for me to find the treasure. When I would find, he would say, 'Someday this treasure will belong to you.' But then comes the fire, and I don't get the chance to find. My father dies. He is a brave man. He dies saving the others. I have to leave, and I never have the chance to find my treasure."

"That's a sad story," Katie said as a shiver ran through her. She wasn't sure if it was the cold or her sympathy for the child Anna once was.

Anna nodded. "It is a terrible thing when a child loses parents, a terrible thing."

"I know," Katie said with an unexpected catch in her voice.

Anna caught Katie in an intense stare. "You do know," she observed, as her soft, gnarled hand reached out and swept Katie's cheek like a feather.

Anna's tender sympathy brought an unwelcome mist of tears into Katie's amber eyes. She looked up at the swaying trees to keep the tears from spilling over.

"Come," Anna said with renewed energy. "I have suddenly an idea. A memory and an idea."

Katie brushed away her tears and followed Anna as she walked briskly toward a dense grouping of thick trees. They were heading farther into the forest, in a direction Katie had never gone.

She followed for ten or more minutes, struggling to keep up with the old woman, who moved now with surprising energy. The dying light overhead worried Katie. She had to get Anna to turn back.

For a moment, Katie lost sight of Anna, then she spotted her up ahead. Somehow the woman had managed to scramble up onto a wide, flat rock. A shard of golden pink sunset bathed her in a sort of glow. She seemed to be looking down at something.

"Anna, we have to go," Katie urged, hurrying to the rock.

The woman didn't appear to hear her. Her gaze was fixed on the sight before her.

Leaping up onto the rock beside Anna, Katie gasped.

Before her were the charred remains of Pine Manor.

One stone outer wall still stood, three stories high. Swirling stone flowers adorned the curves of its tall windows. The once-grand windows had now simply become openings through which poured the soft, golden rays of the sunset, illuminating the otherwise shaded space behind the wall.

The trees here were younger and smaller than elsewhere in the woods. Obviously the older trees had been burned and these younger ones had come up in their place. They let in more light than the ancient, dense woods Katie and Anna had passed through on their way to this spot. Looking up, Katie could even spy a patch of brilliant sky.

Some inside walls still stood, making a rough map of the ground floor. On one wall, the frame of a burned painting still hung. A massive stone fireplace stood alone in the middle of the wreckage. A charred stone stairway was still visible where the front steps had been, although they'd sunk into the ground. In front of it stood a rusted door grating made of fancy ironwork.

To Katie, the iron door seemed like a faithful servant guarding its magical, ancient kingdom, somehow unaware—or unwilling to admit—that it had been destroyed.

"We were very happy here," Anna murmured. "Very happy." Bending to grip the rock, Anna climbed down and headed toward the remains of Pine Manor. Katie followed, mesmerized by the sight.

Together, they walked into the center of the manor. What a grand place it once must have been.

Katie turned in all directions, looking for any clue to the whereabouts of the golden angels. Anna, too, searched, running her hands along the walls.

Three converging lines? Where could they be?

It was all pretty hopeless. Anything the fire hadn't destroyed was warped and faded from time.

Katie turned and noticed something that made her heart beat hard. "Anna, look!" She pointed to the ironwork gate at the front entrance.

The top half was all busy, curved scrollwork. But at the midpoint it changed into three lines that met at the middle of the gate. Three converging lines.

Anna and Katie ran to the gate. "Yes, under the steps!" Anna cried excitedly. "A perfect hiding place. Perfect!"

But the steps were sunk deeply into dirt. The top half lay slanted and covered in moss. The bottom half had pushed the ground down, making a deep indentation in the earth.

"We'll never get under there," Katie said unhappily.

Anna didn't hear her. She had already lowered herself to the side of the stairs and knelt, clawing the ground at the base of the stone steps with her bare hands. "We will find," she spoke confidently, indifferent to the dirt that caked her arms and front as she dug.

Katie hopped down beside her. "Anna, we can come back tomorrow," she said, kneeling next to the woman. "It's going to be pitch black soon. We won't be able to see a thing. Believe me. It gets so dark in these woods you can't even see your hands."

A lock of white hair fell into Anna's face as she dug ferociously. "No! Anna will find," she said without looking up.

Katie raised her head to the sky. The glorious sunset was fading into a dim slate gray. With the departure of the sun, Katie felt a bitter cold sweep through her. "Anna! We can't stay!" she shouted. "Please! You've waited this long. Tomorrow we'll bring back shovels and work gloves. It'll go faster. What good is the treasure if we freeze to death out here tonight?"

Anna stopped digging and nodded. Wiping the wet dirt on her skirt, she stood. "You make sense, my friend. Let us go."

Feeling relieved, Katie led the way back toward the Angels Crossing Bridge. As they walked, she carefully noted landmarks—fallen trees, odd-shaped boulders, mossy inclines—along the way. She had to be sure she and Anna could find their way back to Pine Manor tomorrow.

Tomorrow she would have her half of the treasure! It wouldn't matter that Uncle Jeff begrudged her or stole from her. She'd have her own money. She wouldn't need him, or Aunt Rainie, anymore. Not ever!

They crossed the bridge and went up the hill. "Where do you live?" Katie asked, suddenly realizing she had no idea where Anna would go when they left the woods.

A mischievous smile crossed the woman's face. "With horses."

"Horses?"

"Yes."

Katie suddenly understood. "In the stable? Have you been sleeping in the stable at the ranch?"

"Yes. Very warm. Horses are good company. Not like people who talk, talk, talk all the time."

"But what do you eat?"

"Oats."

"Horse oats?" Katie asked, grimacing. "Yuck!"

"Is not so bad," Anna said with a chuckle. Then her face darkened. "When we flee Russia, we have nothing to eat for days." She sliced the air with her hand. "Nothing!"

"How horrible," said Katie. In her life, she'd never missed more than one meal at a time. She couldn't imagine being that hungry.

As they walked, Katie wondered what to do about Anna. She couldn't let her sleep in the stable and eat oats. That wasn't right. "Don't you have a home?" she asked.

"No go back to home," Anna said harshly. "Home, no good. Daughter think Anna is crazy."

They silently walked together until Katie spied a light shining through the trees. It came from the stable's outside light. Thank goodness they'd made it. Now, what should she do about Anna?

I know, Katie thought. During the spring and summer, guests stayed at the ranch in a cozy, rustic guest house called The Pine Manor Ranch Inn. It was closed now for the winter, but Katie knew that the lock on the back door was broken.

"I've got a good place for you to stay, and I'll bring you some real food," Katie told Anna. "I'll come for you right after school tomorrow. We'll bring shovels and picks. Maybe I can convince my friends to help."

"Good," said Anna with a smile. "I am glad to share my treasure with such a true friend."

"No problem," Katie replied.

The light from the stable guided Katie's footsteps like a welcoming beacon. She quickly led Anna out of the woods.

"There she is!" an unfamiliar female voice shouted the moment Katie and Anna stepped out of the woods.

Katie turned sharply toward it.

A blond woman in a long mink coat was running toward them. Beside her were two burly men in heavy white pants and matching khaki jackets.

Katie didn't know what to do, what to think. Stunned, she watched as the men gripped Anna by both arms. Anna squirmed like a wild animal. "No!" she shouted at the men. "No!"

"Mother!" the blond woman shouted harshly. "Please! We've been looking everywhere for you!"

Anna looked to Katie. "I give you my treasure!" she shouted. "I give it to you! Promise to find it!"

12

"Aren't you coming to the hospital with me today?" Christina asked the next day in school.

"Oh, man," Katie said, pounding her fist on her thigh. "I completely forgot." They stood in front of the cafeteria door, letting other students pass them on the way in.

"We're practicing for the show at the nursing home, remember?" Christina said with a frown. "How could you forget?"

"I just forgot. Sorry," Katie said. Rhonda Lynbrook passed her. Their eyes met and Katie looked away. Soon she'd have the money for that trip to Washington. She'd never have to listen to snobby remarks from someone like Rhonda ever again. "Listen, Christina, I can't come today," she said, stepping closer to Christina. "I have to go find Anna's treasure."

"What?" Christina yelped. "You heard what her daughter said last night. Anna is crazy! There is no treasure!" Moments after the two men grabbed Anna, Mr. and Mrs. Kingsley, Alice, Ashley, and Christina had come running to see what was going on. The men were from a private psychiatric hospital where Anna had been living, enrolled there by her daughter. Anna had walked out without telling anyone, and her daughter had been searching for her for over a week.

"I know what she said," Katie mumbled. Anna's daughter lived in the next town over, Miller's Creek. The police over there had been notified. After Mrs. Kingsley's call, they'd alerted the daughter to look for Anna in Pine Manor woods.

"I don't think Anna is crazy," Katie insisted. The night before, she'd told Christina and Ashley all about the burned down Pine Manor. "Her treasure has just got to be hidden under those steps."

"Well, maybe," Christina conceded. "But can't you wait? Ashley, Molly, and I can go with you on Saturday."

"No," Katie said, shaking her head. "The Washington trip money is due tomorrow, Friday. I need it today."

"But the show's next week," Christina said.

Katie gazed into her friend's clear blue eyes and sighed. Sometimes she thought Christina was quite looney with all her New Age beliefs, but she was also the most completely sincere person Katie had ever met. She deeply respected that about Christina. It made it hard for Katie to refuse her anything. "All right," she said reluctantly, "I'll come."

That afternoon, Katie watched the assembled children sing their songs. They *did* look angelic with their faces sweetly upturned, singing out, not one bit self-conscious about missed notes or fumbled words. She poked

Christina and nodded toward a pretty dark-haired girl with large, luminous dark eyes. "Why is Marta back here?" she questioned, worried that the little girl's leukemia had returned.

"Just tests," Christina assured her. "She's fine. They're only checking to make sure."

"Good," Katie said, and quietly crossed her fingers.

"Excellent!" Christina told them enthusiastically when they'd finished. "Let's try 'I Love Music' now! Remember, I want to hear lots of pep on this one."

With bright, sparkling eyes, the kids launched into the upbeat song. Katie smiled at the way Chu-Lian wriggled her slim shoulders back and forth as she sang. So cute!

But soon Katie's mind wandered. Everything was under control here. Christina and the other volunteers really didn't need her. She could slip out and still have time to go look for Anna's treasure before dark. She could get a start on it, anyway.

She backed toward the door as Ms. Baker was coming in. "Would you please tell Christina I had to go," Katie whispered to her.

"Okay," she said. Ms. Baker turned to listen to the sweet singing voices.

Katie burst from the room, clattered down the wooden steps, and hurried out onto the front porch. As she headed along the path, she couldn't stand the delay anymore. Her feet flew as she ran toward the bus stop.

"Left at the bridge. I'm pretty sure," Katie spoke aloud to herself. She'd crossed the covered bridge, barely aware of it except as a landmark telling her she was heading toward the burned-down Pine Manor. She leaned a moment on the handle of the waist-high shovel she'd borrowed from the stable. With the shovel, she'd get at that treasure more quickly. With a deep, determined breath, she picked up her shovel and continued.

From there, she walked swiftly, following the landmarks she'd memorized. It wasn't long before she stood at the boulder and gazed down at the ruined manor house. Like a lost, ancient city, it stood silently, holding treasure just waiting to be uncovered.

Going directly to the sunken steps, Katie found the place where Anna had started digging. With her full weight, she heaved the shovel into the hard dirt. *Clang!* The shovel hit something hard!

Yes!

There was definitely something down there.

Grimacing with the effort, Katie committed every bit of her strength to digging. She dug frantically, as if her life depended on it. She dug with such determination that she barely noticed the icy rain that began to pelt her. When she did notice, she smiled. *Good. The rain will make the dirt softer, easier to dig.* All the better for her.

After an hour of digging, Katie's hands were raw. Two fat blisters had formed along the top of her right palm. On her left hand, the space between her thumb and forefinger blazed bright red. Sticking the shovel into the dirt, she pressed her burning hands against her cool, damp jeans to sooth the stinging.

The rain was coming harder now. A cold rivulet found its way down Katie's back, sending a chill through her.

For a moment, she considered leaving. But the moment

passed in a wave of new determination. "I have to get those golden angels," she said, turning back to her work.

After another ten minutes of digging, something white appeared through the dirt. Tossing away the shovel, Katie knelt in the mud, clawing at the dirt. "Come on, come on," she said, speaking breathlessly to the white surface.

She placed her aching hands on the cool white surface. Ran them up, then down. *This is just one more step*, she realized. The steps were sunk so deeply into the dirt, she might never reach the end of them.

Sitting back on her heels, Katie ran a mud-caked hand along her forehead, smearing herself with dirt. An awful, bone-deep exhaustion grabbed hold of her. This was hopeless. The treasure might very well be under there, but she'd never be able to unearth it. Maybe someone with heavy machinery could do it, but she couldn't.

Soaked and miserable, with bent, defeated shoulders, Katie got to her feet and picked up her shovel. Dragging it behind her, she turned from the disappointing Pine Manor.

When she reached the boulder where she and Anna had stood the day before, she stopped and looked back at the dismal, ruined place. "Sorry, Anna," she said quietly. "I tried. Maybe Pine Manor is just a bad-luck place."

Katie's gaze swept forlornly across the ruins. Suddenly she froze, barely daring to breathe.

On the far side of the building stood a leafless white birch tree, seeming to shiver in the rain. Three trunk stems shot out of a single base.

Three lines converging at a single spot.

Swept through with renewed energy, Katie gripped her shovel and leaped from the boulder. With feet pumping, she ran to the birch. She danced with light, excited steps in front of the branches. Where could it be? Where would Anna's father have put his trunk of golden angels? Her eyes darted from tree trunk, to quivering branches, to the roots.

And that's where she saw the rectangular depression in the rain-soaked dirt. It looked like something had been buried close to the surface but had sunk deeper with time. It was a perfectly chest-sized shape.

Katie seized the shovel and dug. It took only minutes to shovel away the wet dirt.

A box appeared. A lovely dark wooden chest inlaid with carved designs of lighter, golden wood. It was roughly the size of a small microwave oven.

With the shovel blade, Katie hacked at the dirt around the chest until it seemed loose enough. Then she knelt and pulled at the chest with all her strength. The box pulled free so suddenly, it threw Katie back onto the ground.

She hit her shoulder blade on a root, but she didn't care. She had it! She had the treasure she'd asked for!

Frantic with excitement, Katie worked her fingers into the dirt-encrusted clasp. "Open," she cried. "Open, please!"

But the chest lid wouldn't budge.

13

Katie dropped the shovel and heaved the heavy chest onto the boulder overlooking Pine Manor. It was no use. She couldn't carry the chest and the shovel. She'd have to leave one behind. And it certainly wasn't going to be the chest.

The rain was tapering off, but the overcast sky made it hard to judge the time. It had to be getting late, though. Katie knew she had to move to make it out of the woods before dark.

Holding the chest in place with one hand, she banged on it with the other. "Open!" she shouted again in frustration. No matter what she tried—hitting the clasp with a rock, prying it with a thick stick—she was unable to force the chest open. Her only choice was to carry it back to the ranch. There, Ashley and she could use the tools at the ranch to unlock it.

She scooped the chest back into her arms, staggering back a step under its weight. *Well, what did I expect?* she told herself. Solid gold angels were going to be heavy.

The heavier the better, really. But making it out of the woods would be difficult. The chest weighed so much.

Katie moved along, setting the chest down from time to time to rest the aching muscles of her arms. A cold wind whipped her wet clothing, and her teeth chattered. Her hands felt shredded and fiery. The last bout of digging was more than they could endure.

Yet she had her treasure. She *had* it! A fierce pride bloomed inside her. She'd gone after the treasure—she'd asked for it, and she'd uncovered it with her own hands. Never again would she have to suffer the humiliation of Uncle Jeff's grudging support. She was free of his cheapness forever.

She felt elated. Triumphant.

Continuing on with the precious chest, she put one foot in front of the other, until the Angels Crossing Bridge came into view. *I'll take a break on the bridge*, she told herself as an incentive to keep moving forward with her heavy load, even though her body longed to stop and rest.

Soon she could hear the roar and rush of the creek as it surged along under the bridge. She wanted to block it out. The sound was too soothing, too lulling. She didn't want to feel dreamy right now. All her energy had to stay focused on the task of carrying the heavy chest.

With her arms about to burst, Katie approached the entrance to the bridge. Excited at the prospect of rest, she quickened her pace.

"Oh!" Katie cried out as she tripped over a rock in her path. She was thrust forward. The chest flew from her arms. "Nooooo!" she yelled as she hit the ground and slid, her empty arms spread out in front of her.

Quickly up on her elbows, she helplessly watched the chest tumble end over end down the embankment next to the bridge. To Katie it seemed to go in slow motion as it was thrown from rock to root, bouncing on its own corners and finally sliding into the creek.

Katie winced as an explosive pain shot up her right leg. "My ankle," she moaned, writhing around to clutch it. "Oh! Ow!" As she touched it, the pain in her ankle grew worse.

She had to get the chest.

She had to get home.

With a surge of willpower, Katie pulled herself to her knees. She'd have to stay off her ankle and put all her weight on her other leg.

On her knees, she crawled to the edge of the embankment. The top edge of the chest was visible above the swirling white water foaming around it. *Okay. No problem*, she told herself. She'd get down the embankment, fish the chest out of the creek, and continue home.

It would be slow going, but she could manage. Toward the end of the trip she'd have the lights from the ranch to guide her, and it probably wouldn't be pitch dark until she was nearly out of the woods. She could do it.

She got into a sitting position and began pushing herself down the embankment. Tall weeds swished against her soaked jeans as she slid past. *No, no*, she thought impatiently. This way was too slow. It would take forever. It would be better to get to her feet and hop. Without any weight on her bad ankle, she could probably make it.

Kneeling forward, she pressed down on the earth in an effort to push herself up. Her arms waving for balance, she made it up, leaning entirely on her good left leg. As she fought for balance, her right foot touched down to the ground.

She screamed as a searing pain burned its way up her leg, starting at her ankle. "Ahh!" she cried out in an agony-filled moan. Her right knee buckled and pitched Katie forward.

Her right hand hit first. Instantly it was aflame with a horrible stabbing sensation, as if someone had thrust a knife into her hand. She yanked it back, recoiling at the horrible surprise.

A long coppery line slithered through the tall wet weeds, sliding rapidly toward the creek.

A snake.

She'd been bitten by a snake. Shaking all over, she turned her hand and examined the hideous two-pronged marks in her palm. They throbbed and seemed to pulse before her horror-filled eyes.

What if it was a poisonous snake?

A rush of dizziness forced Katie to rest her cheek on the cold, weedy ground. She realized her heart was pounding. She could hear its pulse in her ears. Pounding. Pounding.

The sound grew so loud, it drowned out the feeling of pain. No more pain in her ankle. No more pain in her hand.

The chest. She had to get the chest.

Forcing her head up, she saw it in the creek. Water washed over it.

The pain came back, full force.

Katie rested her head again. A wet, dirty clump of hair fell into her open mouth. Its wetness felt good in her dry mouth.

Pain filled her. She had to make it go away. She needed the sound of her heart. She had to find the pounding.

There it was! Pulsing at her temples. Pounding. Pounding. Pounding. Steady. Comforting. The sound of her own heart beating.

The pounding filled her. The pain was going away.

Everything was going away.

14

Katie's eyes opened just a slit. White, artificial bulb light poured into them.

"You're safe now," said a soft, warm voice. A strong hand cradled her head.

Forcing her eyes open wider, Katie found herself staring into a lovely, glowing face. Deep, lavender-blue eyes smiled back caressingly. Lovingly, the hand lowered Katie's head onto a wooden surface.

The bulb light grew brighter as the shining woman backed away. Katie realized that she was lying on Ashley's front porch. The woman was so tall, the top of her head nearly brushed the ceiling.

Katie reached up, not wanting the woman to leave. She felt no pain. It had all somehow vanished. But she was frightened. It was night. No one knew she was out here. She tried to stand, but her body wouldn't move. She was too weak. "Help me. Please," she whispered, pleading, her voice dry and cracked.

"Help is coming," the woman said confidently.

A strange calm came over Katie. The woman seemed so sure that she'd be all right. As the woman turned to leave, Katie saw wings at her back.

Impossibly huge, shimmering white wings.

Everything would be all right, Katie told herself as she fell back into blackness.

"Katie! Oh my gosh! Katie!"

Katie's eyes opened again. Ashley stood over her, pale with worry.

The pain was back. Oh, no! It was back stronger than ever! NO! It hurt so much.

Ashley knelt beside Katie. "What happened? How did you get here? What happened?"

"A snake," Katie whispered hoarsely. "Bit me."

That was all she could manage. Saying that much had used up all her strength.

Ashley put her hand on Katie's head. "Mom!" she shrieked at the top of her voice. "Dad!"

Katie was dimly aware of the front door opening. "Oh, no!" she heard Mrs. Kingsley cry.

The next time Katie awakened, she was in a hospital room. It was dark except for light coming from the hall and some that filtered in from the streetlights outside. A monitor over her bed blinked with neon green lines. Tubes in her arm were connected to an intravenous drip bottle on a stand beside her bed.

Her ankle still throbbed and her hand was sore, but the awful dizziness was gone.

A sputtering sound startled Katie. Turning, she saw

that Uncle Jeff was asleep in a chair nestled in the corner of the room. He gave a sharp cough, and his steely blue eyes opened. "Ah, you're awake," he noted.

Katie nodded, shrinking back into her pillow. He'd probably be angry with her. This hospital must cost money.

"How do you feel?" he asked, coming to the side of her bed.

"Not great," she replied. "Better than I did."

"Snake got you, huh," he said evenly. "Did you get a look at it?"

"It was coppery."

Uncle Jeff nodded. "Copperhead. They've got one nasty bite. You're lucky you got to the ranch in time."

"In time?"

"Copperhead bite can be deadly if you don't get to it in time," Uncle Jeff told her. "You're a strong girl to get back to the ranch with a snake bite and your ankle like that." He nodded toward Katie's ankle, which was hidden beneath the sheet. "That thing's swollen to twice its normal size," he said. "The docs were more worried about the snake venom in your system, though. They'll see to the ankle later."

Katie remembered the angel who had helped her home. She'd have died if the angel hadn't brought her to Ashley's.

Abruptly, Uncle Jeff turned from Katie as a coughing fit seized him. He was red-faced when it sputtered to a close. "Sorry," he apologized when he turned back. Katie recalled the coughing fit he'd had the day of the kitchen fire.

"You okay?" she asked weakly.

"Sure, sure," he said gruffly, wiping his mouth with a white handkerchief. "This danged cough! Thought it would go away after I left the mines."

"You were a miner?"

"All the men in my family were. I did it for fifteen years. From the time I was seventeen till when I was thirty-two. By then my lungs got so bad I had to do something else or die. Can't say I miss it. It's rough work. Rough work. The cough comes on me now and again." A quick, self-mocking smile flashed across his creased face. "Rainie says it comes when I'm upset. I think she's crazy, though."

"Are you upset now?" Katie dared to ask.

"Sure I am," he barked.

Uh-oh. Here it came. The hospital bills.

"Well, not really. Not anymore. After all, you seem okay now. You should have seen your aunt, though. She was so upset I thought she'd pull every frizzy blond hair out of her head. I sent her home to get some sleep."

Uncle Jeff started coughing again.

"You should check that out," Katie said when he finished. "It might be serious."

"Naw, it's nothing. I don't have time for doctors," Uncle Jeff said as he settled on the end of the bed. "I've got to keep working. That kitchen is going to cost a fortune, and there wasn't as much money in ol' Stony Mae as I'd thought."

"Stony Mae?" What was he talking about?

Uncle Jeff snickered quietly. "Yeah, that's what my sister, Helen, and I called the angel we built out in the woods behind the house. We filched some wet cement from my father when he was making that path that leads to the house. We went to the woods and built an angel of wood and cement."

"Just for fun?" Katie asked.

Uncle Jeff nodded. "It was Helen's idea, of course. She was crazy about angels. Ever since the day she found that Angels Crossing sign in Pine Manor woods. You found it in the barn, didn't you?"

"Yes," Katie said. "I know which one you mean."

"Well, ever since she found that, it was angels, angels, angels with her. She wanted to build this thing. She was my big sister, so I did what she told me and helped her with it. It was fun. We named her Stony Mae. And we built a hollow section, a secret compartment in the middle of her."

"What for?" Katie asked.

"Helen was always putting all manner of strange things in there, lockets, photos, old newspaper clippings. When she got married and moved away, I took it over. I started stashing extra cash I saved inside Stony Mae."

Uncle Jeff's words came back to Katie. *I'll take the money from her. She'll never know the difference.*

He'd been talking about Stony Mae!

He hadn't been planning to steal her trust money at all!

"I'm so sorry," she blurted. Even though he knew nothing about it, Katie felt she owed him an apology.

"No need to be sorry," Uncle Jeff said gently, misunderstanding her meaning. "I'm sure you didn't plan to go out and get yourself bit by a snake. I'm just relieved that you're all right."

"You are?" Katie asked, genuinely surprised.

His eyes widened and his brow furrowed. He appeared surprised at her surprise. "Of course I am, Katie." He took her hand in his rough one. "You're our girl, aren't you?"

Happy tears sprang to Katie's eyes. Their girl. It sounded good.

"Aren't you?" he prodded with a gruff tenderness.

"I guess," she replied.

He squeezed her hand. "Of course you are. I may be a cranky old fool, but I think about you as if you were one of my own daughters."

"Really?" Katie could hardly believe what she was hearing.

"Really."

15

Katie went home three days later. Although she was well enough to leave the hospital, the snake poison had left her in a weakened state, and her ankle, while not broken, was badly sprained. The doctors told her aunt and uncle that the thing she needed most now was rest.

Mostly she slept during the day. In the evenings, she sat in her room, warmed by the electric heater, and listened to the steady drone of hammering coming from below. Mel and Uncle Jeff were building a new wall in the kitchen with pieces of plywood.

Wow, Mel is working, Katie thought with a grin as she settled back in her pillow. *What a concept!* Maybe some good had come from the fire, after all.

Aunt Rainie had taken a leave from her job at the beauty parlor, where she did shampoos and cleaned up. Three times a day she brought Katie meals on a tray.

"Your friends have been calling, sweetheart, but I told them you're too weak yet to talk," she told Katie one evening as she laid the tray on her lap.

Katie looked at the greasy canned beef hash on the plate. How she hated it. But Aunt Rainie thought it was the best meal on earth. And her own cooking was much worse. "Thanks," Katie said. "You're right. I don't really feel up to talking."

It was true, her body felt heavy and her mind sluggish, as though even when awake she were really half asleep.

"Katie, hon, I'm not clear on some things," Aunt Rainie said as she lifted Nagle in her arms and petted him. "How *did* you make it out of the woods?"

"An angel brought me," Katie said, not seeing any reason to say otherwise.

"An angel?" Aunt Rainie murmured thoughtfully. "Well, I suppose you might have been delirious, what with all that awful snake poison pumping through your system."

"No," Katie insisted, picking up her fork. "It *was* an angel. I saw her."

Aunt Rainie frowned skeptically. "I suppose it's possible . . . but . . . I guess we'll never know," she said, placing Nagle on the bed.

Katie knew, though. She'd seen the glowing face, the awesome wings. An angel had saved her life.

"The other thing I was wondering is, what on earth were you doing in the woods by yourself?" Aunt Rainie asked.

"Looking for gold."

"Gold?"

"I wanted money for . . . stuff."

"Like the Washington trip?"

Katie nodded. "And other things. I figured if I found

the gold I wouldn't be such a burden on you and Uncle Jeff." She figured that was still the truth, only put in more pleasant terms.

Aunt Rainie smoothed the top of Katie's pillow-tossed hair. "Aw, honey, you're no burden. I wish we had more to give you. You bring such life to this house, we're glad to have you."

"Thanks," Katie said, surprised by the small lump that had formed in her throat at her aunt's kind words. "Do you mean it?"

"Sure I mean it." Aunt Rainie squeezed Katie's hand and Katie squeezed back. "But why on earth did you think there would be gold in those woods?"

"Someone told me there was. An old lady I met in the woods. And it was true, too. I found a trunk, but I couldn't open it. Then it dropped into the creek when I fell."

"Imagine that," Aunt Rainie said, her eyes growing wide with interest. "A real trunk. I wonder what was in it?"

"Gold," Katie stated confidently. "I'm sure of it."

Aunt Rainie sighed. "Gold," she repeated softly. "Think of that. You almost had your hands on a chest of gold. Wouldn't that have been nice for you. Like a fairy tale."

"Maybe I can go back and find it," Katie considered, the idea entering her mind for the first time.

Her aunt's face clouded over. "I don't know about that. You're still very weak. Even gold isn't worth risking your life for."

"In stories people always risk their lives for gold," Katie argued.

Aunt Rainie smiled and smoothed Katie's blanket. "That's stories, honey. Besides, I like stories where people risk their lives for love better. I think those are much more interesting. Gold might be lovely, but love . . . well, love is . . . it's . . . everything."

By the second day, Katie's head cleared and instantly she felt restless. Taking her notebook out, she looked over her story, "The Fire." She decided to change the name to "The Girl Who Found a Fortune."

> Melinda and Goofy escaped through the tunnel with their gold. "Whew!" Melinda said. "We made it." Goofy barked in reply. Melinda looked at the trunk of gold in her arms. She had risked her life to get out of the burning building with the gold.

A picture flashed into Katie's head. She saw herself struggling with the box, muddy and wet. And she envisioned what she must have looked like as she tried to make her way down to the creek on her rear end, struggling so hard to get to the chest of gold in the water.

In those moments, the chest had seemed so utterly, totally important. The most important thing in the world.

But it hadn't really been. She'd been wrong about Aunt Rainie and Uncle Jeff. And she might have died trying to get that chest.

Brushing back her auburn hair, Katie continued to write.

*   *   *

If she hadn't been carrying the gold, she could have run through the tunnel much more quickly. Why had she been so foolish? What did she think the gold would really do for her? Would it make her dreams come true? Maybe. Maybe not. Melinda needed to think about it. She needed to give it a lot of thought.

By Thursday, Katie returned to school, using a cane to support her bad ankle. Molly, Christina, and Ashley hovered around her, carrying her books, making sure she felt all right. "Today is our last rehearsal before the nursing home show," Christina told her that day at lunch. "It's all right if you don't come, though. No one expects you to."

"No, I'll be there," Katie said, leaning on her cane to help herself into a cafeteria chair.

"Are you sure?"

Katie nodded. "After nearly a week in bed, I'm going bonkers. I need to do something."

Ashley and Molly joined them at the table. Ashley set down a tray of macaroni and cheese in front of Katie. "Here you go," she said. "Neon yellow school cheese, like nothing else ever seen on this planet."

Katie looked at the bright noodles and laughed. "Thanks."

That afternoon, with Christina's help on and off the bus, they arrived at Children's House. Getting up the stairs to the second floor was a struggle, but Katie managed by taking each step slowly.

Once in the day room, awash with bright winter sun,

Katie found herself very glad to be where she was. The kids were so beautiful as they sang.

She watched brave, bright-eyed Marta—so cheerful— Chu-Lian, and the others. They all had so much spirit.

A picture of Clara formed in Katie's mind. She remembered her conversation with the old woman. In a flash of understanding, she knew how Clara felt about the children. Katie recalled her words. "Children are the most beautiful, precious things on earth."

Katie wondered if old Clara would be strong enough to see the show. And she thought about Anna. She was safe with her daughter, but was she happy? She probably still wanted that treasure.

The treasure. Had it been washed downstream? It was probably too heavy to go very far. It had to be still in the creek.

Katie owed it to Anna to get the chest to her, she decided. With whatever share Anna gave her, she'd help Uncle Jeff and Aunt Rainie build a new kitchen. She'd missed the deadline for the trip to Washington, but there was still time to help her aunt and uncle. After the way she'd misjudged them, she felt she owed them that much.

As Katie and Christina got off the bus that afternoon, they met Molly and Ashley at the entrance to the ranch. They were both on horseback.

"We rode out to meet you," Ashley said. "How was practice?"

"Great," Christina replied. "It's going to be great show."

Katie looked at her friends and asked the question that had been on her mind all the way home on the bus. "Will you guys come look for the treasure with me?"

"Now?" Molly asked, glancing at the fading, late-afternoon sun.

"You can't go into the woods with a sprained ankle," Ashley objected.

"That's why I need your help," Katie insisted. "We still have an hour or two of light."

"Katie, give it up already," Molly said impatiently. "You almost died because of that treasure. How badly do you really need it?"

"It's not for me," Katie told her. "This time it's for my aunt and uncle and for Anna."

"How would you even find Anna?" Ashley questioned.

"Through her daughter. The Miller's Creek police must have her name and address."

"It wouldn't hurt to take a look," Christina said. "I'll go with you." Ashley and Molly agreed to go, too.

"Thanks, guys," Katie said sincerely.

A twig snapped sharply under Katie's cane as she entered the woods.

"Want to lean on me?" Ashley offered, stopping to wait for Katie, who lagged slightly behind her friends.

"No, I'm okay. I'm just moving kind of slow." Katie managed with her cane until they came to the hill just before the Angels Crossing Bridge. There, she needed Molly, Ashley, and Christina to support her as she made her way up the hill.

When they reached the top, Katie scanned the area, looking first to the place where she'd last seen the chest. No sign of it.

"Look! Over there!" Molly shouted, pointing to the

other side of the bridge. "What's that thing stuck between those two big rocks?"

"Yes!" Katie shouted. "That's it! That's it!" The water had pushed the chest upstream, under the bridge, but two rocks now blocked it from moving any farther.

"Let's go!" Christina yelled, dashing wildly down the hill.

Molly took off after her. Ashley followed, but stopped halfway down the hill to check on Katie.

"Go ahead," Katie urged her. "I'll catch up." Ashley ran after the others as they continued racing down to the creek. Katie hobbled down the hill as fast as she could with her cane.

She met up with her friends as they were hurrying back up from the creek and crossing the bridge. "We can't reach it from this side," Christina explained with breathless excitement.

Ashley waited for Katie at the entrance of the bridge. "I guess you're in luck, after all," she said with a smile.

"I guess so," Katie agreed, taking Ashley's arm.

As Ashley and Katie struggled down to the water's edge, Christina and Molly leaped out onto two large, nearly-touching rocks. The chest bobbed wildly in the space between them.

As she came closer, Katie could see the trapped chest more clearly. The powerful rush of the water kept the chest from floating backward, and the rocks kept it from going forward. It was locked into the space between the rocks, continually smashing into them.

Christina crouched low and, grimacing with the effort, gripped the chest and pulled with both hands. "Oh! Oh, no!" she cried out as the weight of the box caused her to totter forward. She fought desperately to regain her balance.

"Gotcha!" Molly cried, her arms waving in an effort to catch hold of Christina's arm. Molly gripped her sleeve, pulling Christina even farther forward. The abrupt movement made the chest slip from Christina's hands.

Katie gasped as the chest plunged back into the creek once again.

At almost the same moment, Molly and Christina pitched forward, splashing down into the icy water.

"Oh!" Molly screamed, standing up in the creek. "It's freezing!"

"The chest!" cried Christina, splashing around in search of it. "Where is it?"

"There!" Ashley pointed to a small pool of bubbling water.

The chest had sunk into the creek, pulled into the icy waters by the treasure inside it. Tugging and pulling, Molly and Christina dragged it up again. Grunting with the effort, they brought the chest to the water's edge.

"Here it is," Molly said as she shivered miserably. Washed clean by the creek, the chest's silky polished wood gleamed in the dappled sunlight filtering through the thick pinewoods.

"I hope this is worth it," Christina added miserably as water cascaded from her hair. "I'm sooooooo cold!"

"I'm sorry you fell in, but it'll be worth it," Katie said confidently. "Really."

One quick glance at the chest made her smile. Finally a lucky break. The chest's lock dangled loosely on one small nail. The repeated bashing it had received on the rocks had sprung the lock.

Katie knelt, her hands trembling as she reached to open the chest.

Slowly, she lifted the lid, anxious to see the golden treasure inside.

When Katie looked into the chest, her mouth fell open. Her eyes saw, but her mind couldn't make sense of the sight in front of her. "What?" she uttered in bewilderment. "What?"

16

"Well," Christina said carefully. "It *is* a golden angel. Technically speaking, Anna was right."

Katie stared hard at the small, feather-light golden angel in the palm of her hand. It had a pinecone body and an acorn head, both painted gold. The gently curving wings, also painted gold, were made from the dried peels of an orange. The delicate angel blew a fragile, tiny hand-carved wooden horn. At the back base of the angel, an acorn cap formed a holder in which a small, birthday-sized candle was held in place by a puddle of its own burned wax.

"It's a candleholder. Actually it's very pretty," Christina observed.

Katie glared up at her. She was in no mood for optimism or positive thinking. This was a disaster!

She shook her head in disbelief. *This* was the treasure? This! The chest was full of the angels—about fifty of them, she guessed—all nearly identical, though ever so slightly different. These were the golden angels?

"I can't believe this," she muttered again.

"Well, it's not really that surprising," Molly said in a practical tone. "I mean, come on. Anna was pretty nutty. You knew that."

"She wasn't nuts," Katie murmured, still staring at the pinecone angel. Sure, maybe a little strange—the way she dressed, wandering around out in the woods, sleeping in the stable, and all—but . . . not crazy.

Everything she'd said to Katie seemed sane. At least Katie had thought so. Yet obviously she'd been wrong. Anna thought this was a treasure. These worthless pinecone angels! Apparently she'd been crazier than Katie realized.

But—wait—something didn't make sense.

Why was the trunk so heavy?

"There's something hidden under these angels," Katie said excitedly, digging through. "There's got to be!" Her hand slid onto something smooth. Yes! Here was the gold, hidden under the pinecone angels. Wrapping her fingers around it, she pulled it up.

"A rock," she said glumly, eyeing the polished stone, roughly the size of a baseball. Looking back into the chest, she pushed aside the angels. The chest's bottom was lined with polished rocks. They were pretty but didn't look at all valuable.

"I'm freezing," Molly complained, her teeth chattering.

With the help of her cane, Katie struggled to her feet. "Let's go," she mumbled glumly as she moved up the hill.

"Don't you want the chest?" Ashley asked.

"What for?" Katie asked.

"Anna might want the stuff," Christina suggested.

"And if she doesn't, you could sell the angels at the holiday crafts fair at the hospital next week. You'd make a few dollars, at least. I bet people would buy these angels."

"The chest itself is nice, too," Ashley pointed out.

"I'll take the rocks if no one wants them," Christina added. "They're pretty."

"Okay," Katie agreed. "You're right. Let's take it. After everything we've gone through to get it, we might as well."

Ashley and Christina lifted the trunk, each taking one end. Without any more discussion, they headed up toward the Angels Crossing Bridge and back to the ranch.

That evening, Molly went home, but Katie and Christina stayed at Ashley's for supper. When Aunt Rainie came to the ranch to pick up Katie, a look of amazement came over her face when she saw Ashley and Christina carrying out the chest. "Is that . . . is that the treasure?" she gasped.

"Sort of," Katie told her, rolling her amber eyes in disgust. She opened the car door and pushed the front passenger seat forward so Ashley and Christina could put the chest into the backseat. "It's what I *thought* was the treasure, anyway."

Katie thanked her friends for their help and said good-bye. "See you at school tomorrow," Ashley said, waving. "Don't be too bummed."

"I'm not," Katie said. "Just disappointed."

As they drove away from the house, Katie reached

back into the chest and showed her aunt one of the pine-cone angels. "Can you believe it?" she asked.

"What a dear thing," Aunt Rainie said. "So sweet."

"I suppose," Katie grumbled, relocking her seat belt. "But it's not treasure. It's not going to get us a new kitchen."

Aunt Rainie glanced at Katie. "You wanted to help with the kitchen? What a lovely thought. Thank you, dear."

"You're welcome . . . for nothing."

"It's not nothing. Your sweet intention is not nothing, hon."

"I can't believe that the lady I met thought this was a treasure," Katie grumbled, shaking her head at the bewildering fact. "She wanted this so badly, she was willing to live with the horses and be out in the cold and rain until she found it. I guess she was kind of wacky after all."

"Maybe not," Aunt Rainie said thoughtfully as they turned out of the ranch drive and onto the main road.

"What do you mean?" Katie asked.

"Maybe it's a treasure to her."

"How could it be?" Katie asked.

Aunt Rainie smiled gently. Rain began to dot the windshield, and she flicked on the wipers. "Sometimes memories can be our dearest treasures."

After school the next day, Katie had a meeting with the *Writer* staff. "Everyone's really excited about our upcoming D.C. issue," Sally told the kids who'd assembled around the table. "Katie, your story is going to be on the front page."

"Uh, Sally, I was going to talk to you about that after the meeting," Katie said, wishing the subject hadn't come up in front of the entire staff. She'd hoped she could privately tell Sally to reassign the story, but now it seemed wrong not to say anything. "I'm not just late with the money. I can't go," she said, speaking quickly. "Someone else will have to write my story."

"I can do it," Rhonda volunteered, casting a gloating smile at Katie.

"What are *you* going to write about?" Darrin asked Rhonda snippily. "About what everyone was wearing at the Kids Conference in Washington?"

Katie shot him a puzzled look. She wasn't used to backup from Darrin.

"Kids are interested in that sort of thing," Rhonda snapped defensively. "I have it all planned out. I knew she wouldn't be able to go."

"Oh, yeah? How did you know that?" Darrin challenged. "Are you psychic?"

"No, you have me confused with Miss Horoscope over there," Rhonda said smugly, nodding toward Christina. "You don't have to be psychic to know that Katie was lying. Her family doesn't have the money to send her. Everyone knows that."

Katie leaned across the table and faced Rhonda. "So what if they don't, Rhonda?" she asked as the heat of her rising anger warmed her cheeks. "Is that some kind of crime or something?"

Rhonda looked away. "Oh, give me a break. I never said that."

"You act like it *is* a crime, or something to be ashamed

of. But it doesn't bother me. Money and clothes aren't the only things I think about."

Rhonda folded her arms and glared at Katie. "Oh, shut up," she muttered.

"Hold on," Sally interrupted. "I'm confused. Katie, what are you talking about? You paid."

"No, I didn't."

"Yes, you did. Last Friday there was an envelope on this table marked 'Katie Nelson, Washington trip,' and inside was a hundred dollar bill. I assumed someone dropped it off for you because you weren't well enough to come to the meeting," Sally explained.

"A hundred dollar bill?" Katie questioned.

"Yeah," Sally confirmed. "I have your train ticket to Washington in this envelope with all the others. All I'm missing from you is a signed permission slip."

A puzzled smile formed on Katie's lips as she took the permission slip Sally offered to her. "Cool," Katie murmured, completely bewildered.

"Didn't you know about it?" Sally asked.

Katie shook her head. "I have no idea where it came from."

Sally shrugged. "Maybe your guardian angel left it," she said jokingly.

"Maybe," Katie agreed, thinking it could well be true.

After they left the meeting, Christina put her hand on Katie's arm. "I think it was Molly," she said.

"Molly paid for my trip?" Katie asked, bewildered.

"I think so. She told me she had a bunch of money in a bank under her bed, and she didn't know what to do with it."

"Wow," Katie said. "Wow."

"I don't think she wanted you to know," Christina added. "I got the idea she wanted you to think an angel paid it."

"I *did* think that," Katie admitted. "But I'm glad you told me."

Christina smiled. "Sometimes friends can be angels."

17

Katie stood at her bedroom window and watched the trees sway uncontrollably in the wild wind. Clouds blocked out the stars and moon. Something banged below her window. Looking down, Katie saw a metal garbage can bounce off Aunt Rainie's parked car. The wind had tossed it right into the air.

What a night to have to go out, she thought, turning away from the window. But it was the evening of the show over at the nursing home, and she had to be there.

"Are you ready to go, hon?" Aunt Rainie called from outside her door.

"Almost," Katie replied. "One minute."

Reaching under her bed, she pulled out her good black flats. She wasn't one for dressing up, but tonight was special. She'd put on her best blue corduroy pants, a turtleneck, and a velvety red vest.

As she bent over to slip on her shoes, Katie's eyes fell on the chest of pinecone angels. She'd tried finding Anna through the Miller's Creek police, but they hadn't been helpful. They said they couldn't give out her daughter's address or phone number. They wouldn't even tell her Anna's daughter's name.

Katie felt stumped. She tried calling her married cousins in Miller's Creek—Aunt Rainie and Uncle Jeff's daughters—but they didn't know anyone who fit the description of Anna and her daughter.

Her cousin Maria had laughed. "If the daughter was wearing a fur coat, we don't know her. There's a section of Miller's Creek that is pretty well-to-do, but unfortunately we don't know anyone over there."

Since she couldn't find Anna, Katie gave Christina the polished rocks and decided to sell the pinecone angel candleholders at the hospital crafts fair as Christina had suggested. Some of the money would go to the hospital, which was a good cause to donate money to, and the rest she'd give her aunt and uncle to put toward the kitchen repairs. It wasn't the same as buying them a whole new kitchen, as she'd hoped, but it would help a little.

Because she had a ride from Aunt Rainie tonight, Katie had decided to bring the chest to Children's House and leave it in the crafts closet until the crafts fair the following weekend. She could put it there after the show. That would be easier than taking it on the bus while she still needed her cane.

Without the rocks in it, the chest was light. Still, it was difficult to pick up, unbalanced as she was by her achy ankle. But by getting to her knees, tucking the chest under one arm, and pulling up on her cane with the other, she was able to pick it up.

Hobbling carefully down the stairs with the chest,

Katie met Aunt Rainie in the living room. "Thank goodness Mel and your uncle put that plywood in place," Aunt Rainie said as she pulled on her bright blue woolen coat. "That tarp wouldn't have lasted tonight. It would have come flying right off in this wind."

"Is a storm coming?" Katie asked as she took her winter parka from the coat closet.

"I wouldn't be surprised," Aunt Rainie said. "At least the folks at the nursing home don't have to travel to the show."

"That's true," Katie agreed. "They all live right there at the home. And the kids are all at Children's House; we just have to get them across the street. And their parents are coming to see the show, so they'll drive."

Katie and Aunt Rainie walked toward the rarely used front door, the only entrance to the house now that the kitchen door was gone. "We're going," Aunt Rainie called to Uncle Jeff and Mel, who were busy stapling bright pink insulation material to the new kitchen wall.

"Have fun," Uncle Jeff called back, not looking away from his stapling.

"Funny," Aunt Rainie said as she turned the knob on the front door. "Working on this kitchen has brought Mel and Jeff together closer than they've been since Mel was a boy. Who'd have thought something so wonderful could come out of something as terrible as a fire?"

Katie nodded. Things sure did work out strangely, in ways a person could never imagine. She was learning that more and more these days.

Aunt Rainie opened the door. The wind grabbed the door, banging it hard into the house. "Good heavens!"

she cried, putting her hands over her curly blond perm to protect its style. "This is unbelievable!"

A paper bag blew past Katie's face, and she ducked to avoid it. Katie had to struggle against the wind to reach the car. A blast of cold air caught her off guard and made her drop her cane. Just in time, her aunt caught her under the arms and helped her into the car.

The ride to the nursing home was a wild adventure. A flying newspaper plastered itself to the windshield, forcing Aunt Rainie off the road to remove it. A plastic garbage can blew into the road. Aunt Rainie swerved and missed it by inches. With a deafening crack, a tree limb split and fell into the road several yards ahead of them, causing Aunt Rainie to bring the car to a screeching stop.

Despite her gulps of fear and gasps of surprise, Katie felt as if they were on an exhilarating ride at an amusement park. By the time they arrived at the nursing home, Katie was in wonderful spirits, excited and enthused about being out on this strange night. As they walked into the nursing home, she grabbed her aunt's arm in surprise. "Look!" she cried, pointing to the sky.

A bank of dense cloud cover had parted as if blown apart. The parted clouds revealed an immense orange moon lying close to the horizon. Stunned, Katie gazed up as the wind whipped her hair.

"A hunter's moon," Aunt Rainie said, gazing up. "It lights the night. You sometimes see them this time of year."

"I've never seen one," Katie said in an awestruck voice.

Aunt Rainie squeezed her shoulder. "Well, now you have." As she spoke, the wind blew the clouds together again, and the moon disappeared from view.

Inside the nursing home, Katie went straight to the social room. Christina was getting the kids seated in a horseshoe of folding chairs in the center of the room. Helping her were Ms. Baker and several other volunteers, including Molly's boyfriend, Matt.

Looking up, Christina noticed Katie and waved. She looked pretty in a short purple velvet dress and matching tights. Her flowing wheat-colored hair was loosely caught up in a knot at the top of her head.

Katie waved back and smiled at the kids, who were all dressed up for the event. Marta wore a large black bow in her short hair. Chu-Lian had on a bright flowered jumpsuit with a ruffled collar. The boys looked sweet with their hair neatly combed.

The elderly residents of the home were starting to file into the social room. Aunt Rainie went to assist a woman with a cumbersome walker.

Katie smiled at Clara, who came in pushed by her beautiful companion. The old woman smiled at Katie and clasped her hand. "Thank you and all the other young people for this show," she said. "You have no idea how much I've looked forward to this. Bless you."

Clara's friend smiled radiantly at Katie.

"You're welcome," Katie said. "I hope you like it."

"I'll love it," Clara said as her friend began to push her once again.

"She *will* love it," the friend told Katie as they found seats and joined the growing audience.

At that moment, the large chandelier in the middle of the room flickered. The room was bathed in a soft, brownish light. "Uh-oh," said the head nurse, Ms. McCrain, coming into the room. Katie looked at her and their eyes met. "We wouldn't want a power failure," she said to Katie. "But this is exactly the kind of weather when we get them."

"Why?" Katie asked, worried.

"Tree branches fall on power lines," the nurse explained. Katie remembered the branch that had fallen in their path on the way over.

In the next minute, the lights came on at full power once again. Katie imagined a tree branch bouncing off a power line but not breaking it. "Let the lights stay on, at least for the show," she whispered out loud, hoping the angels would hear.

She hurried to the center of the room to help with the kids. "Remember, we sing, 'I Love Music' after we sing 'Let's Go Fly a Kite,'" Christina was telling them. Katie straightened bow ties and hair ribbons as she listened with one ear to the trees banging on the windows.

In less than five minutes, the kids were ready to begin singing. When Katie turned around, she saw that the room was jammed with people. The older people in wheelchairs—including Clara—were up front. Others sat in chairs behind them, and standing against the walls were the beaming parents of the sick children. Katie realized that this was not only a wonderful moment for the kids and the older people but for the worried, weary parents as well.

Christina stepped in front of the kids. "Hello, everyone," she said brightly. "Thanks for coming to our show. The kids are ready, so let's begin."

She turned and gestured to the kids, giving them their signal to start singing.

At that instant, the entire room plunged into total darkness.

18

At first, total silence swept the room. It was broken as Katie's cane clattered to the ground. Startled by the sudden darkness, she'd let it slip from her hands. Now she supported herself on a folding chair.

The unnatural silence gave way to a buzz of frightened murmurs from the adults and sudden outbursts of fearful tears from the children. A line of brilliant light pierced the blackness and revealed Nurse McCrain holding a flashlight. "Stay calm, everyone. Everyone stay where you are. There's no need to panic."

Katie felt a hand on her shoulder, but the blackness around her was so complete that she couldn't even see the person standing beside her. "Get the angels from the car," the person whispered softly.

Whose voice was it? Katie turned and peered hard into the darkness, reaching out. The person had silently moved away. She felt nothing.

Katie started to walk in the direction of Nurse McCrain, who was standing in front of the doorway.

"Just stay put," the nurse was saying. "The lights will probably come back on in a few minutes."

In the flashlight beam, Katie saw the kids all looking wide-eyed and scared. "We can sing something," Christina suggested, turning to them. "How about 'I Love Music'?" She started to sing. Marta sang with her, but the other kids were too scared of the darkness. Some were still crying. Christina's valiant attempt wasn't going to work.

Katie slipped out the door. Red exit lights glowed in the dark hallway, guiding her to the front door. As soon as she stepped out into the parking lot, the howling wind almost threw her back against the door. *My cane*, she remembered, gripping the door handle.

She hadn't needed it to get this far. *I guess I don't need it anymore*, she realized. When she pressed her weight down on the sprained ankle, it felt a little weak but not painful.

Outside, she saw lights on at the hospital. Otherwise, everything was dark, even the illuminated sign in front of the hospital and the streetlights. The power failure had obviously hit the entire area.

With her head bent against the wind, Katie found Aunt Rainie's car and took the chest from the backseat. Why was she doing this? She didn't know. But the person who had told her to bring them in had sounded so sure of herself. It was strange—almost like Katie couldn't *not* do it.

Katie carried the chest inside. When she got back to the social room, several other flashlights were being held by the members of the nursing-home staff, but the light was still dim and confined to the flashlight beams. Nurse McCrain was making an announcement. "Our generators have been turned on in the bedroom wing. We have enough power to light that section, but not this wing of the building. Staff members will assist you in returning to your bedrooms."

"What about the show?" asked a crackly, indignant voice. Nurse McCrain waved the beam of her light in that direction. It was Clara.

"Sorry, Clara," Nurse McCrain said. "The show will have to be postponed."

A groan of disappointment came from both the children and the nursing-home residents.

"I know it's disappointing, but we'll have it another evening," Nurse McCrain told the group.

Katie's eyes fixed on Clara's disappointed face. She slumped in her wheelchair. Katie wondered if Clara would live to see the postponed show. She noticed Clara's companion standing beside her. A tear ran down her lovely face.

Ms. Baker clicked on a flashlight and walked toward the children. "Will parents please come up one at a time and claim your child so we can bring them back to Children's House in an orderly fashion?"

The children hung their heads. What a disappointment. And they'd been so excited.

"Wait!" Katie called out, as an idea suddenly came to her. "I have a chest full of candles here. If we lit them all, I bet we'd have enough light."

"Candles could be a fire hazard," Nurse McCrain objected.

Katie opened the chest and held one up to the nurse's flashlight beam. "They're small, birthday-sized. There are fifty of them. If it was someone's fiftieth birthday it wouldn't be a fire hazard, would it?"

"If it were my birthday there'd be over a hundred," Clara called out, looking lively again.

Nurse McCrain laughed. "All right. We'll see how long the candles last. We can have a shortened version of the show."

"Yeah!" the kids cheered.

Adults came forward and helped Katie light the candles. They each took a candle and found a spot for it. "Great idea, hon," said Aunt Rainie as she came to light a candle.

"You didn't tell me to get the candles?" Katie questioned. Her aunt shook her head.

Soon the room was awash in gentle light. "It's like a picture. A beautiful picture," Christina said as she came alongside Katie.

"You didn't tell me to get the candles, did you?" Katie asked.

"No," Christina replied.

"Strange," Katie murmured, half to herself.

Christina returned to the kids and led them in a rousing rendition of "I Love Music." Their young voices blended as if they'd been trained to harmonize, although they hadn't been. One song smoothly followed another. The crying kids forgot their fear as they gave themselves over to the joy of performing.

Katie looked around at the elderly people so softly illuminated by the candlelight. Some sang along. Others smiled gently, their hands pressed together in delight. Clara beamed with a special light of her own. Katie had never seen a person so transformed by inner joy.

The look on Clara's face was a sight so moving, Katie knew she'd never forget it, not ever. Her companion, too, smiled with radiant joy.

As the performance continued, Katie kept a careful watch on the candles. They couldn't last much longer. Yet they showed no signs of burning out.

A soft hand touched Katie's. She looked down at an old man sitting in a chair. "It's like Chanukah," he said happily. "The light shouldn't be lasting this long, but it is."

"Yes," Katie replied, realizing he was right. "It *is* like that."

Matt came forward and separated the kids into two groups, passing out red cowboy hats in preparation for singing "Achy, Breaky Heart." Christina walked over to Katie. "Come with me to get the leis for the Hawaiian song," she said. "I left them out by the front desk."

"Okay," Katie agreed. They went out into the dimly lit hallway and headed for the desk.

"Your cane," Christina noticed. "Where is it?"

"I don't need it anymore," Katie replied. "My ankle doesn't hurt."

"Cool," Christina said. They walked up to the desk and found the shopping bag filled with colorful leis. "I can't believe how long those candles are lasting," she commented happily.

"I know," Katie agreed. "A man told me it reminded him of Chanukah."

"Like the oil lamps in the ancient temple that burned for eight days?" Christina said, her eyes widening at the idea. "I suppose that's true. It's like our own miracle."

From the social room they could hear the children singing the last verse of "Achy, Breaky Heart."

"We'd better get these leis inside," Katie said. With the bag of leis in her hand, Katie followed Christina back into the room.

As they walked through the swinging double doors, Christina gripped Katie's wrist hard. "Do you see what I see?" she whispered.

Katie's jaw dropped but no sound came out. All she could do was nod and stare in awestruck wonder.

19

Behind every pinecone angel stood a magnificent eight-foot golden angel holding a blazing torch that filled the room with radiant light.

Some were female angels, others male. Each wore a flowing gold robe that emanated golden light. Their wings were spread wide and shimmered like sunlight bouncing off a wave.

No one else seemed to notice them.

Since the leis hadn't come, Matt started the kids on the next song they'd planned, "Let There Be Peace on Earth." The kids' angelic voices filled the hushed room.

Overwhelmed by the splendor of the angels and touched to the heart by the sweet, clear singing, Katie felt her eyes fill with joyful tears. The elderly people beamed at the children, happily transfixed.

Wiping her eyes, Katie looked to Clara. Her wrinkled face was bright with joy, but slowly her head drifted over to the side, and she slid back into her chair. Her companion waved her graceful hand down the length of the old woman's face, and when she took her hand away, Clara's eyes were closed.

Katie stared, not understanding.

The companion quietly wheeled Clara toward the door. Was Clara dead? Katie moved toward them, needing to know. As she approached the companion, breathtaking wings unfolded from the woman's back.

"It was her time." The woman spoke in a voice Katie recognized. It was the same voice that had told her to get the angels. Now, although the angel didn't appear to speak, Katie could hear her voice in her own mind. "She forced herself to live just for this show. But she couldn't have held on any longer. She died as she lived, joyfully. Thank you."

Katie nodded, her eyes riveted on the angel. Everyone was so focused on the show, no one seemed to realize that Clara appeared to be moving herself out the door. No one but Katie could see that she was being pushed by an angel.

20

With colorful leis around their necks, the kids sang their Hawaiian song. Marta and Chu-Lian performed a hula dance. When that was done, they sang "Puff the Magic Dragon" and then invited the audience to join in as they sang their final number, "Bridge over Troubled Water."

The voices of young, old, and in-between mingled. As they sang, the golden angels slowly faded out of sight. With the fading of each angel, a candle burned out. By the last verse, only about ten candles were still lit and the light was dim. Then, one by one, the last ten angels disappeared and the room was once again plunged into darkness.

Yet the sound of heartfelt applause filled the black void.

Flashlight beams snapped on to illuminate the children as they bowed.

"Wonderful." Nurse McCrain spoke. "Thank you, children, so much. Now everyone please stay seated until staff members can assist you back to your rooms."

Ms. Baker asked parents to come to the front to collect their children.

Katie saw that everyone seemed quiet, yet intensely happy. Even though they hadn't seen the angels as Christina and she had, they all seemed to know they'd been part of an extremely special evening. Something inside them had been deeply touched. They'd been touched by angels, but they'd also touched one another, shared something wonderful.

Holding a flashlight in one hand, Christina draped her other arm over Katie's shoulder. "You were right," she said. "Those angels *were* worth finding."

Katie nodded. She wouldn't be able to sell them at the crafts fair now, not after tonight.

"I'll start to gather them up," Christina offered.

By the red light of the exit sign, Katie noticed a woman coming through the swinging doors. She wore a long mink coat. It was Anna's daughter. In the next second, Anna came through the door. She appeared more well-groomed than when Katie had last seen her. Her white hair was pulled tightly up into a bun, and she wore a long brown coat. Her face was solemn and unhappy. Katie rushed over to her. "Anna!"

"My friend!" Anna cried, the stern lines of her face melting into a smile.

"Please, young lady," the daughter said, stepping between Katie and Anna. "I'd appreciate it if you don't get Mother all worked up. We have just come to see if Mother would like to live here. Unfortunately we've been caught in this dreadful power failure."

"Then you didn't see the show?" Katie asked, bending around the daughter to speak to Anna.

"No, but I heard the very end of the most beautiful singing. Most beautiful," Anna replied.

As she spoke, the lights overhead flickered and turned on. Katie squinted at the harshness of the ceiling light. "Thank goodness," the daughter huffed.

Katie gripped Anna's arm excitedly. "Anna, I found the—"

Before she could finish, Anna's face flowered with happiness as she looked over Katie's shoulder. Christina was walking toward them with the chest filled with angels. "My treasure!" Anna cried. "You have found my treasure."

"Mother, please don't start with that nonsense again," the daughter scolded.

Anna paid no attention. She rushed ahead to meet Christina. "My angels. My treasure," she crooned, cradling a small pinecone angel lovingly.

"That . . . that's your treasure?" her daughter asked in a bewildered voice.

"Yes, yes!" Anna said. "When I was a little girl in Russia, we had angels of pure gold. Gorgeous. With jewels in them. We brought them out every holiday season. But then the Communists came and we fled Russia. In Russia my father was a count and a fine horseman. In America he found work at Pine Manor as a stableman. He made these angels to remind me of the golden angels back in Russia, to show me that everything was still fine although we had no longer wealth."

"They're very beautiful and very special," Katie said.

"Yes," Anna said, nodding. "Very special. More special than the golden ones we had in Russia, because these were made for me with my father's own loving hands."

"They were buried under the tree," Katie told her.

"Ah," Anna said. "Yes, of course, the three-trunked birch."

"I have the polished rocks," Christina said.

"Yes, the rocks," Anna said, smiling fondly. "My father would say, 'Look, my little Anna. We have jewels, too,' and he would hand to me a rock he had polished. He said, 'Here in America, Anna, we have everything. We are now poor, but we have lost nothing of real value and have gained much.'"

A sadness clouded Anna's face, then she smiled at Katie. "I have no longer a place for these angels, so I give them to you."

"I couldn't keep them," Katie said. "They're your special angels."

"Keep them, Mother," Anna's daughter said with unexpected softness. "I had no idea you were looking for something real. I thought you were—"

"Just a crazy old lady," Anna finished for her.

Her daughter blushed. "I thought you were remembering the treasure your family left back in Russia. I thought you were . . . confused."

"No, not confused," Anna said, holding one of the little pinecone creations to her heart.

"Let me give you some money for the angels . . . to thank you for finding them for Mother," the daughter offered Katie.

Katie waved her hand. "The angels saved our show tonight. That was enough reward."

"No, I insist," the daughter pressed.

"No way," Katie said, shaking her head. "I couldn't take your money, not for helping a friend."

Christina offered to send the rocks back to Anna. "Or I could bring them to you here," she suggested.

"Mother will be staying with me," the daughter said quickly. "I thought she was confused and needed more care than I could give her. But maybe I'm the one who has been a bit confused."

Anna winked at Katie and Christina. "Maybe so," she said with an impish grin. "You girls keep the rocks. And think of old Anna when you look at them."

"Please let me give you a reward for finding this treasure," the daughter insisted again.

"Thanks, but no thanks," Katie said. "I really couldn't take it."

At home that night, Katie worked on the conclusion of her story.

> Melinda realized that the gold she'd risked her life for couldn't buy her what she wanted. She wanted to be loved. And she wanted to feel good about herself, to like the person she was inside. She had those things now. The fortune she'd found was in her heart.

Katie closed her notebook and went downstairs. With a shiver, she entered the chilly living room. Uncle Jeff,

Aunt Rainie, and Mel were watching TV. "What a night, eh, Katie?" Aunt Rainie said with a smile.

"It sure was," Katie agreed. And Aunt Rainie didn't know the half of what had happened.

Uncle Jeff wasn't paying attention to the TV. He worked seriously, writing something on a pad.

"What are you doing?" Katie asked, craning to see what he was working on.

"What?" he asked, looking up. "Oh, I'm trying to figure how much flooring tile we need for the kitchen. I seem to remember there's a box of old tiles out in the barn. They're a little damaged, I suppose, but we can use them."

"Finish the insulation first," said Aunt Rainie. "It's freezing in here."

"Can't," Uncle Jeff told her. "Can't afford any more right now."

"Spud's got some in the back of his garage," Mel said, referring to his friend. "Maybe I can get some from him." Dizzy wandered into the room and licked Katie's hand. "Hey, I think he likes you better than me," Mel noticed.

Katie shrugged and scratched Dizzy between his black ears.

"Darn!" Uncle Jeff grumbled as the point of his pencil broke.

"I might have another one in my jacket pocket," Katie said, going to the hall closet. She reached in and dug in the pocket of her parka. She pulled out not a pencil but a roll of money.

"What the . . . ?" Katie unfolded the tidy bills. Five hundreds!

Anna's daughter must have slipped them into her pocket.

"Did you find a pencil?" Uncle Jeff called to her.

"No, but look!" She held out the bills.

"That's a lot better than a pencil," Mel laughed.

"I'll say," Uncle Jeff agreed. "Where'd it come from?"

Katie quickly explained to them what had happened. "I don't know how to give it back," she added.

"You don't have to," Aunt Rainie said. "The woman obviously really wanted you to have it."

Katie handed it to her uncle. "For the kitchen," she said. "You can buy insulation now."

Uncle Jeff frowned. "No. No, Katie. That money is yours. I couldn't take it. That's not right."

"Yes, it is," Katie said. "Don't I live here?"

"Sure, but . . ."

"Aren't I a part of this family? It's only right. Family members help each other, don't they?" Katie said, keeping her hand extended.

Uncle Jeff took the money from her. "I suppose you're right, Katie. Thank you. It's real sweet of you. You're an angel."

"No, I'm not," Katie said with a laugh.

"Wait," Uncle Jeff said, peeling off one of the hundred dollar bills. "Didn't your aunt tell me you needed a hundred dollars for your Washington trip? Here. I hope it's not too late."

Katie took the bill from him. "No, it's not. It would have been, but Molly paid it. Now I can pay her back."

Folding the bill, Katie put it in her back pocket. She sat with her family and watched TV with them. After one show, she yawned, said good night, and headed for bed.

In her room, she walked to the window. The fierce wind had subsided and the huge orange hunter's moon had reappeared, though now it was higher in the sky. Katie thought of the angels on the moon.

Although they'd been busy and faraway, they'd heard her.

She'd asked for wealth, and she'd received it—the true wealth that lies only in the human heart. The treasure of love.

FOREVER ANGELS

by Suzanne Weyn

Everyone needs a special angel . . .

Katie's Angel
0-8167-3614-6

Ashley's Lost Angel
0-8167-3613-8

Christina's Dancing
Angel
0-8167-3688-X

The Baby Angel
0-8167-3824-6

An Angel for Molly
0-8167-3915-3

The Blossom Angel
0-8167-3916-1

The Forgotten Angel
0-8167-3971-4

The Golden Angel
0-8167-4118-2

The Snow Angel
0-8167-4119-0

Ashley's Love Angel
0-8167-4202-2

Available wherever you buy books.

Troll